"You make me sick, stealing from your own school," he said.

"But—but I'm not! I'm not stealing anything!" Christine stammered. She held out her hands, as if to show that she was telling the truth.

Andy raised his eyebrows skeptically. "Oh, yeah? Then what exactly are you doing in the boys' locker room? An interview for 'ABC Sports'?"

Christine felt humiliated. She was torn between keeping her cover and proving her innocence. She finally decided to tell him the truth. "OK," she said. "I'm here trying to catch whoever is stealing the gym equipment."

Andy was silent.

"I'm a detective. A private investigator," Christine added.

Andy laughed at that. "A detective? You?"

Christine became angry. "Why is it that every time I say I'm a detective people laugh? Why is it so funny?"

Andy dug his hands into his pockets, still smiling. "I don't know. It just is."

Bantam Sweet Dreams Romances
Ask your bookseller for the books you have missed

Private Eyes

Julia Winfield

BANTAM BOOKS

TORONTO · NEW YORK · LONDON · SYDNEY · AUCKLAND

RL 6, IL age 11 and up

PRIVATE EYES
A Bantam Book / December 1986

ISBN 0-553-25814-1

Published simultaneously in the United States and Canada

*Bantam Books are published by Bantam Books, Inc. Its trademark,
consisting of the words "Bantam Books" and the portrayal of
a rooster, is Registered in U.S. Patent and Trademark Office
and in other countries. Marca Registrada. Bantam Books, Inc.,
666 Fifth Avenue, New York, New York 10103.*

Printed and bound in Great Britain by
Cox & Wyman Ltd, Reading

O   0 9 8 7 6 5 4 3 2 1

Private Eyes

Chapter One

"Page seventy-eight. This is a new world record for me," Christine Harter said from her chair. She lowered the book she had been reading. With a characteristically dramatic gesture, she covered her eyes with one hand and peeked through her fingers at her elegant slate gray cat curled up on her bed.

"Phiz, I am absolutely positive the stepson did it," she added contentedly.

Her cat showed no sign of interest. In mock-anger Christine threw a tattered catnip mouse at him.

"Fine. If you don't want to listen, I'll tell Rondo and Speckler how I solved the mystery," she declared. She lined up a stuffed walrus and tiger on her bed against the wall, then stood in the middle of the room to appraise them. Abruptly, Christine crossed her arms and began to pace.

"You see," she began, pushing a stray lock of sandy blond hair behind her ear, "Reggie isn't really Clarke's son at all. I see you're surprised, but it's true." She stopped her pacing and nodded at Rondo. She saw that Phiz had begun a bath—a sure sign of disguised interest—and decided to include him in the lecture as well. "OK, Phiz. Now look sharp and pay close attention, because I'm only going to go through this once."

She went back to pacing the room. "Where was I? Oh, yes. Reggie. Lillian, Reggie's mother, had an affair with Arthur when she was married to her husband, Clarke, and she passed Reggie off as Clarke's son. And now that she's dead, Reggie will inherit all of Clarke's money."

Suddenly Christine bounced onto the bed and knocked the stuffed animals on their faces. Startled, Phiz dug his claws into the bedspread. "But!—Arthur, who's married to Caroline, found out that he's Reggie's real father, and he told Reggie. And if he told anybody else, Reggie wouldn't inherit. So Reggie killed him."

Speckler and Rondo were speechless, and the cat just blinked lazily.

"Boy. You guys are such duds." Christine shook her head disgustedly. "OK. Need proof? Now remember, Reggie is staying with Arthur and Caroline for a while. Listen to this." She tucked her legs under her and opened *The Turlaine Incident* to read aloud.

The door of the breakfast-parlour opened, and Reggie strode into the room. His manner was that of a powerful man in control of his surroundings. Caroline remarked inwardly, not for the first time, how dangerous and cruel Reggie could look, his dark, handsome face and charming smile belying his cold, steely eyes.

"Morning, Auntie," he said carelessly, seating himself at the table.

She stiffened involuntarily but managed to nod her head curtly.

The young man noticed her response and laughed softly. "Don't worry, Auntie dear. I assure you I'm being dutifully mournful about poor Mother passing away. I'm positively desolate." With a grin he snapped open the *Times* of London and began reading.

3

"You wretched, unfeeling beast," Caroline gasped. "You are so delighted to be inheriting your father's money at last, you don't care whom you hurt."

The two stared at each other for a tense moment, over the damask-covered table.

The door opened again, and Arthur Turlaine entered, his usually strong and confident air visibly strained by grief. He regarded Reggie thoughtfully for a moment and cleared his throat.

"Reginald, I've been going through your mother's things. There's something I think you should know. Will you please come with me to the library?"

Reggie's eyes narrowed. Then he stood up to follow Arthur out of the room.

Christine closed the book with a snap and tapped it on her knee. "See, that's where Arthur tells Reggie the truth," she told the animals. "It's *always* the handsome stepson."

She stretched backward over the edge of her bed. Her Mickey Mouse sweatshirt pulled up to expose her bare midriff. She mumbled, "I guess I'm getting better at detecting, you guys."

She had figured out *The Turlaine Incident*

in record time. It usually took her at least half the book to solve the crime, but she always got it right.

"Chriiiiii—is," Mrs. Harter called from downstairs.

With a quick glance at her bedside clock, Christine rolled backward off the bed, scrambled to her feet, and ran to the head of the stairs.

"Yes, Mom?" she answered.

"Time to set the table, dear." Mrs. Harter appeared at the foot of the stairs, wiping her hands on a dish towel. She smiled. "Or are you in the middle of a case?"

Christine cocked her head to one side and squinted her eyes against imaginary cigarette smoke. "No, sweetheart," she said through clenched teeth. "I got this case in the bag."

Mrs. Harter chuckled as she made her way back to the kitchen. Christine went into the bathroom to wash her face and hands and to brush her fluffy hair.

"Miss Harter," she said, pointing her hairbrush at her image in the mirror. "We understand you've done some impressive work on the Turlaine incident." She shifted slightly to one side, and cast her eyes down modestly. "Oh, inspector, it was really very simple. You see, Reggie Turlaine would have inherited millions. In my experience it's always the handsome young man, and it's always for money."

Christine studied herself as she spoke. Would freckles, sandy blond curls, and a dimpled smile help her image as an ace detective? She raised her eyebrows skeptically.

"Hardly," she said with disgust as she turned away. "Detectives shouldn't have freckles. No one takes you seriously if you have freckles."

Muttering gloomily, she stamped hard on each step as she went down the stairs.

"Christine! Stop pounding down those stairs."

"Sorry, Mom," Christine said as she stepped into the warm, fragrant kitchen. Before she knew what was happening, a pair of strong arms had grabbed her from behind and lifted her into the air in a clinch.

"Danny! You jerk!" she shrieked at her older brother as he bounced her up and down. "Put me down, you gorilla!"

"OK, Beanie." Daniel Harter said. He was laughing as he released his hold on her. She stared up at him, still gasping.

"You two can roughhouse outside, not in here," Mrs. Harter said. She smoothed her

6

graying blond hair with one hand. "You're in high school, not preschool."

"But, Mom," Christine began indignantly. "I'm not roughhousing." She glared at her brother and sat down. "Danny is the culprit here, not me. And you would know that if you had made a careful observation of the scene."

"Cut it out, Chris," Danny said, poking her in the ribs. He ducked out the door, before Christine could turn on him.

"Boys—especially senior boys—are so immature it's disgusting," Christine said. She picked up a carrot stick from the bowl on the table. "Mom," she continued, crunching on the carrot, "do you think there's a place in this male-dominated world for female detectives?" She looked earnestly at her mother. "I'm serious."

Beverly Harter sat down across from her daughter, and thoughtfully fingered the amber beads at her throat.

"Well, honey," her mother said, "it's true that detectives traditionally have been men. Of course, there are fictional women detectives. But it seems to me that all you need to solve mysteries is brain power." She grinned. "And we know men don't have a monopoly on that."

"No way!" They smiled at each other. Then Christine grew sober.

"Mom, I really *want* to be a detective." She picked up a stack of supermarket coupons and began shuffling through them. She looked up at her mother. "But I don't know how to begin."

"Christine," Mrs. Harter said, reaching across the table to take her daughter's hand. "I know you want to be a detective, but you're only a sophomore in high school. You want to start now?"

Christine nodded. "I figure if I can start building my reputation now, by the time I graduate from college I'll be a famous detective, and I can start working full-time."

"I see you're determined to try this. Go ahead and be a detective, if you want, but don't expect mysteries to drop into your lap as often and as conveniently as they did into Nancy Drew's," her mother told her. "And don't make a nuisance of yourself poking into other people's business. If a case comes along, fine, but don't go looking for trouble."

"Oh, Mom—"

Mrs. Harter looked sternly at Christine. While you're in my house, don't get involved in anything illegal or dangerous. If you do, young lady, your career will be short." She stood up and went to the stove. "Stick to the books for now, honey. I think you'll be better off. Now will you please set the table?"

Christine stood up and walked over to a cabinet to get the plates.

"And stand up straight, Christine," her mother added.

The family sat down to eat as soon as Mr. Harter arrived home from work. Christine wondered whether Danny was going to monopolize the conversation again with his college plans. Lately, he talked about nothing else. Right on cue, Dan cleared his throat. "I guess I'll try law school after college," Dan said, looking at his parents casually.

Mr. Harter smiled. "That's awesome, Dan."

Christine choked as she swallowed her milk. She finally managed to gasp, "Dad!"

He smiled at her. "What's wrong? Isn't that the right word, 'awesome'? I hear you kids use it all the time."

Danny shifted uneasily in his seat. "Sure, Dad, but you don't . . ." His sentence trailed off, and he shrugged.

Christine tried to explain. "What Danny's

9

trying to tell you, Dad, is that fathers aren't supposed to say 'awesome.' "

Mr. Harter shook his head. "I don't see why not. I just want to communicate with you kids. I'm trying to be hip."

Christine and Danny tried to choke down their laughter. Christine put her fork down carefully. "Then don't say 'hip.' No one's said 'hip' since the seventies."

Mr. and Mrs. Harter both raised their eyebrows, clearly amused. "The Dark Ages!" Mrs. Harter said.

"Well, I still think Dan's wanting to go to law school is an awesome idea," Mr. Harter said, helping himself to more mashed potatoes.

Christine could tell that her parents really were thrilled by the idea. They would be proud to have a lawyer in the family. She sighed audibly.

"What's wrong, honey?" her father asked.

Daniel cut in. "She's just stewing over her own career plans. We've been talking about someone besides her. That's what's wrong with her."

Christine sighed again. "Danny, I wouldn't dream of taking you out of the limelight. You go ahead and be a lawyer." She paused to glance at her mother. "You never know—my

10

career may come in handy for you sometime," she said cryptically.

Her father took the bait. He leaned back in his chair and loosened his tie. "Why's that, Christine?"

Danny answered for her. "Because she wants to be a detective. Can you believe it?" he asked, laughing. "What a joke!"

Christine narrowed her eyes and waved her fork furiously at him. "Look, Danny. Detectives have ways of finding things out about people. And detectives sometimes tell other people what they know. So I'd be nice to me if I were you."

Danny shifted uneasily in his seat and shot a couple of sidelong glances at his parents.

Mrs. Harter threw her white napkin into the middle of the table. "Truce. Please return to your corners, kids. No more fighting at the table."

"What's this all about, anyway?" Mr. Harter asked, leaning forward to look more closely at his daughter.

Christine felt a little nonplussed. Her father had always encouraged her to pursue her goals. But she couldn't believe they'd take her seriously this time.

She drew in her breath. "Dad, you know I always solve the mystery stories I read, right?"

Her father nodded.

This is going to be tough, Chris thought. She continued. "So I think I could really be a good detective. I can put together details. I understand motives. I think I could psych out the criminals." She looked hopefully at her father.

Mr. Harter looked at his wife. Mrs. Harter said, "I told her it was OK as long as it didn't infringe on her schoolwork or place her in dangerous situations."

Christine saw her father raise his eyebrows. "Do you mean to tell me she's going to start detecting *now*?" he asked. He turned back to Christine. "Young lady, real-life mysteries are quite a bit different from detective novels. I hope you realize that."

"Sure, Dad—"

He held up his hand to silence her. "I don't know about this. I thought teenage girls were supposed to be interested in *boys*, not criminals."

Danny burst out laughing, and Christine blushed, feeling tears start to well up in her eyes. She knew her parents worried because she didn't have any dates. Christine assumed it was because she spent so much time reading—even during lunchtime she usually had a paperback propped up in front of her in the cafeteria.

"Come on, Dad, cut it out. Detectives don't have time for romance," she said, not looking up. But she looked guiltily at her mother. They'd had a couple of heart-to-heart talks about boys. And Mrs. Harter knew that Christine wasn't as casual about boys as she liked to pretend.

Her father shook his head, feeling guilty that he'd hurt his daughter unknowingly. "I find it hard to believe that a fifteen-year-old detective is going to have a lot of cases," he said, changing the subject.

"Actually," Danny said, "there is one mystery at school you might try solving."

Christine nodded eagerly. "What is it?" she asked. She carefully avoided looking at either of her parents.

He put down his forkful of potatoes. "Well, some equipment has disappeared from the gym during football practice. It's happened a couple of times. Some shoulder pads and helmets are gone. Expensive stuff."

"How long has this been going on?" Mr. Harter asked.

"Have the police been notified?" Mrs. Harter asked.

Danny shook his head. "It started three weeks ago, and they haven't called the police yet."

Christine smiled. "Because they think it's a student, right? And they don't want to bring in the police unless it's absolutely necessary."

"Right," Danny said. "How did you know?"

"I'm a detective. Remember?"

Mrs. Harter stood up to being clearing the table. "Will you help me please, dear?" she said to her husband.

"Who, me?" he asked, surprised.

She grinned. "Yes, dear. You."

Mr. Harter dropped his napkin on his chair as he stood up. Christine heard her mother whisper as her parents went into the kitchen, "I think we should let Christine question the first witness in private."

Chapter Two

After school the next day Christine hurriedly stowed her homework in her book bag, stuffed a small notepad in her jeans pocket, and jogged over to the gym at a slow, steady pace. She couldn't wait to start her first case!

When she arrived she found the JV cheer-leading squad well into practice. The captain, Teri Hutchinson, ran over to greet her.

"Chris, hi," Teri said, panting slightly. She and Christine had been friends for years.

Christine said "hi" and looked around at the squad stretching their legs and waving their arms in slow circles. "You're here every day, right?" she asked her friend.

Teri nodded and flipped her long brunette ponytail over one shoulder. "You know I am.

Hey, mind if I hold on to your arm for a minute?" she asked as she stretched one leg up behind her.

Christine tried to hold her steady and continued, "Ever see anybody around the gym who shouldn't be here? Any strangers?"

Teri let her leg drop suddenly and stared at Christine as she pushed her bangs out of her eyes. "What's with the third degree, Christine? Are you playing detective?"

"Actually, I am." Christine replied laughing. "I'm trying to solve the mystery of the stolen gym equipment."

"What?" Glancing quickly around them, Teri took Christine by the arm and led her a few steps away from the rest of the squad. "Chris, no one's supposed to know about that. Coach Keeler told us all to keep quiet about it. Just the people who are at the gym every day know."

Christine was calmly writing in her notebook. "Danny told me last night," she said.

"Oh, well, I guess if Danny told you it must be OK," Teri said. She sounded relieved. "Chris, does Danny ever mention me?"

Christine looked up, smiling. "Why don't I put in a good word for you at dinner tonight?" she suggested.

"Don't you *dare!*" Teri said soberly. Then she smiled. "Anyway, I've got to get back to practice. To answer your question—no, I haven't seen anyone around who doesn't belong here. Good luck." She jogged back to the rest of the cheerleaders as Christine walked to the other end of the gym.

Christine knew that to get to Coach Keeler's office, she'd have to go through the boys' locker room. She'd been so excited to start the case, she had forgotten one small detail: the boys' locker room was off limits to girls. The thought of entering it mortified her.

"What's the big deal here?" she asked out loud. "There's no one in there, after all. Everyone's out at practice." But her words sounded hollow.

Christine looked furtively around her. The locker room door was hidden from view from the cheerleaders, no one would see her enter—but she still felt as though the whole world was watching her.

She knocked timidly on the door, but nothing happened.

She knocked again, a little louder, and pushed the door open slightly. "Anybody there?"

Her halfhearted call was met by a warm

draft of air that smelled faintly of gym socks and soap. Feeling a little bolder, Christine slipped inside and stood with her back against the door. She let her breath out slowly.

Come on, Harter. Where's your professionalism? she thought. She looked around a bit more confidently.

It was exactly the same as the girls' locker room! Christine laughed at herself for expecting an alien world. She pushed away from the door and wandered down the aisles of lockers.

The locker room was large, and it seemed especially large to Christine because she was alone. *I wonder if I'm the first girl to ever come in here?* she thought. She also wondered how many people would be horrified at the thought of her trespassing. She was sure her parents would be.

Christine made her way through the locker room to the "cage"—the corner next to the coach's office that had been walled off by heavy gauge chicken wire on the open side, forming a triangular-shaped room. Since it was sizable and secure, most of the gym equipment was stored there. According to Danny, it was the site of the thefts.

Christine fully expected to find a shiny new

lock on the door, but to her surprise, it was an old and worn-looking one. And it was unlocked. Just as Christine was about to steal into the coach's office for a preliminary examination of it, she heard the locker room door open. Someone was coming toward her!

Horrified, Christine leaped into the cage and pulled the door shut. She flattened herself against one of the walls, behind a box full of basketballs. She recognized Coach Keeler's hearty voice. He was the temporary coach who was filling in while the regular coach was sick.

"Just pick up four more Ace bandages from the cage, would you, Andy?"

"Sure, coach." It was a boy's voice, one Christine didn't recognize.

Christine stayed frozen as the creak of the door and quick steps told her that Andy—whoever he was—was now in the cage with her.

Her view was limited to a small space directly in front of her left eye. A tall, brown-haired boy passed her line of vision. She caught a glimpse of his face, and instantly recognized him as Andy Mellon. He was Danny's age, but she couldn't remember if she'd seen him on the team. Automatically she reached for her notepad to write down his name. At that moment Andy looked around.

Please don't see me. Please don't let him see me, she thought frantically, her heart pounding wildly as she thought of a dozen crazy excuses for being there.

For one tense moment Christine thought he was going to turn and see her. But he only picked up a small box and went back out through the door. Christine drew one cautious breath.

"Here they are, coach," Andy said. From the sound of his voice Christine knew he was just outside the cage.

"Fine, Andy. I've got what I need. Let's go," Coach Keeler said.

"Uh—coach? Do you want me to lock up the cage?"

Christine's heart skipped a beat. Lock the cage? With her inside?

"No, Andy. Leave it."

"But, coach. What about—"

"Leave it, Andy."

Almost collapsing with relief, Christine leaned back against the wall and shook her head. She heard the door shut on the far side of the locker room as the coach and Andy went back to the football field.

Cautiously, Christine eased out from behind the box of basketballs. She accidentally set it swaying. First she steadied it, then tip-toed to the cage door and opened it. She poked her head out, ready to run back under cover in a moment. She was alone again in the locker room.

Satisfied that she could leave the cage, Christine walked over to a bench and sat down to record her observations.

"Coach Keeler insisted that student Mellon leave the so-called cage unlocked. Equipment remains accessible. This investigator could easily have removed a number of items without fear of apprehension."

She chuckled softly. OK, so she *had* been just a little apprehensive. She flipped the cover of her notepad closed. Standing up, Christine decided to turn her attention to the coach's office and walked to the heavy oak door.

"Good thing I found an excuse to come back. Is there anything left to steal?" a voice asked over her shoulder.

Whirling around in a panic, Christine found herself face to face with Andy Mellon.

She tried to remember what her favorite fictional detectives would do in a situation like this, but her mind was a blank. All she could think was that up close, Andy Mellon was a very attractive boy, even furious.

"You make me sick, stealing from your own school," he said.

"But—but I'm not! I'm not stealing anything!" she stammered. She held out her hands, as if to show that she was telling the truth.

Andy raised his eyebrows skeptically. "Oh, yeah? Then what exactly are you doing in the boys' locker room? An interview for 'ABC Sports'?"

Christine felt humiliated. She was torn between keeping her cover and proving her innocence. She decided to tell him the truth. "OK," she said. "I am trying to catch whoever is stealing stuff from here."

Andy remained silent.

"I'm a detective. A private investigator," Christine added.

Andy laughed at that. "A detective? You?"

Christine became angry. "Why is it that every time I say I'm a detective people laugh? Why's that so funny?"

Andy dug his hands into his pockets, still smiling. "I don't know. It just is. Say, aren't you Dan Harter's kid sister?" he asked.

Christine defiantly faced Andy with her hands on her hips. "Yes. Why do you find it so hard to believe I'm a detective? Because I'm a girl? Do you think girls are dumb or something?"

"Easy—easy! Sorry." Andy held his hands up in front of him. "I take it back. I guess I was just surprised, that's all. I never met a girl detective before. I mean, I've never met *any* detective before."

Christine grinned. He sounded sincere.

Andy stared at her, then broke into a wide, beautiful smile. "I wasn't being a male chauvinist, honest," he told her. He had a gorgeous smile and a twinkle in his blue eyes that Christine found hard to resist; then she reminded herself that she was working on a case.

"Well, OK. 'I'm Christine Harter: I try harder.' That's my motto." She walked back to the bench, sat down, and pulled out her notepad. "Mind if I ask you some questions?"

Andy seemed surprised. Then he shrugged and straddled the bench next to her. "Shoot."

Christine tucked a stray lock of hair behind one ear with her pen and then began writing. Without looking up she said, "You're Andy Mellon, right?"

"Right."

"And what connection do you have with the football team? Are you a player?" she asked.

He shook his head. "No, I'm the team manager."

Christine wasn't sure what that meant, but she nodded and wrote it down. "Team manager. Do you have any idea who's taking the stuff?"

"Uh—no. No, I don't." Andy was carefully retying the laces of his sneakers and didn't look at her as he answered.

Christine frowned. "Who has access to the equipment?" she continued.

"Well, you've just proven that just about anyone does—if you include girls who'll go into the boys' locker room," he added, smirking.

Christine smirked right back at him. Then she became serious again. "How come it isn't protected? I mean, it was so easy for me to get in here and get into the cage, no wonder stuff is being taken."

"I know. It bothers me, too. I keep telling the coach we should change the lock—even when the cage is locked stuff is taken. Over the years a lot of copies of the key got made for other players and managers, and all the other teams in our conference have keys, too. We don't really know how many extra keys are floating around. But the coach won't change the lock, and sometimes he doesn't even lock the cage."

Christine put her pen to her lips and nodded. "I heard your conversation with him. Why do you think he does that?"

"He says we've got a better chance of catching the guy if we make it easy. He says the thief might get careless, thinking he can come in anytime and take things," Andy said. He propped his legs up on a bench across from the one they sat on and shook his head. "I guess he knows what he's talking about. He says he's seen this kind of thing happen before."

"He wants to catch the guy himself, doesn't he?" Christine looked at Andy, who smiled ruefully at her and then nodded.

"He thinks it may be someone on the team, right?" she asked.

"Right. How did you know?" Andy looked at her with obvious admiration. "Don't tell me—it's your job as a detective to know these things."

Christine laughed and said, "You're catching on."

The two smiled at each other for a long

moment, until Christine pulled her eyes away and looked down at her notes. She took a deep breath.

"Can you remember the days when the thefts took place?"

Andy thought for a moment. "Let's see. I guess the first one was three weeks ago, probably on a Tuesday. Before we went out to practice on Wednesday, Keeler asked me to get an extra helmet, but there were none in the cage. I had seen them there on Monday."

Christine looked up from her writing. "Helmets? Why would anyone steal helmets? I mean, could you sell them?"

"Well, that's the weird thing," Andy said, rubbing his chin. "I think—this is just a non-professional opinion—" He broke off, grinning at Christine.

She grinned back. Andy was so friendly and easy-going. "OK. What's your nonprofessional opinion?"

Andy furrowed his brow and sighed. "Well, doesn't that sound sort of crazy—stealing helmets?"

"Hmm," Christine nodded. "You mean, this person could be some kind of kleptomaniac?"

"You're the p.i.," Andy replied.

"All right. You said that it could have hap-

pened on a Tuesday. Can you remember anything about that day? Did anyone leave the
field during practice that you know of?" she
inquired.

Andy stood up. His friendly manner suddenly changed. "No—I don't think—I don't
remember," he said briskly. He looked at his
watch. "Look, today's an early practice, and all
the guys will be coming in any minute now."

"Gosh—" Christine jumped off the bench
and stuffed her notes into her pocket. She felt
herself blush.

Andy took her arm, and they started running back through the locker room toward the
door. "Come on, Ms. Detective."

By the time they had rushed through the
door, they were both panting. They leaned
against the wall of the alcove and burst out
laughing. They stood there and watched as
the team came back into the gym from the
field. Danny caught sight of Christine standing next to Andy.

"What are you doing here?" he asked. He
seemed honestly surprised.

Christine said, "I had to stay after, and I
wanted to get a ride home with you, big
brother. Can I, huh? Please?"

He playfully shoved his helmet into her

stomach. "Sure thing, Chris." He walked toward the door through which she had so recently raced.

Christine turned back to Andy. But he was gone. While Christine had been talking to her brother, Andy Mellon had simply vanished.

Chapter Three

Kent, one of the other varsity players, sat in the front seat with Danny on the way home. The two boys talked about nothing but football during the whole ride. Christine sat in the backseat and tuned out their conversation. She stared moodily out the window as they drove down the streets of the quiet New York suburb where they lived.

Christine was both excited and scared about her first case. Just working on it was thrilling, but Christine was also aware that if the thief was someone on the team, then he was probably someone she knew or a friend of her brother's. Stealing from the school was a real crime, and if she solved the case, it wouldn't end as happily as in her favorite novels.

And then there was Andy. Christine felt confused about the case, but there was one thing of which she was certain: she wanted to know Andy better; and her interest in him was no mystery!

"What's the matter with you anyway?"

Christine flinched, jolted out of her reverie by Danny's voice. Her brother was looking back at her from the front seat; they were alone, parked in their own driveway.

Embarrassed, she grabbed her book bag and opened the door. "Nothing. Just thinking," she muttered.

"Pretty heavy-duty thinking, Chris." Danny smiled as he slammed the car door behind him. "Not turning into an intellectual, are you? Pondering the secrets of the universe?"

"Ha, ha. Very funny," she said. Christine turned to her brother, surprised at her own irritation, "People do think, you know. And sometimes—sometimes—they even get lost in thought. Ever hear that phrase, Dumb Jock?"

Danny stared at her, obviously hurt. "Drop dead," he said. He turned toward the house and left Christine alone in the driveway.

She instantly regretted her words. "Me and

my big mouth," she chided herself. She ran to catch up with him on the slate path to their front door. "Danny," she said. She caught his arm, turning him around to face her. "I'm sorry, Danny. Really," she said.

He shrugged. "Forget it," he told her.

"No. Really. I'm just grouchy. Go ahead, call me anything you want. I deserve it," she said, grinning.

Danny grinned back.

"Look. Can I talk to you after dinner tonight? About the case?" she asked.

Danny met her gaze questioningly. "Case? Oh—right." Then he smiled. "That's why you were at school? Then you're really going through with this 'dumb' idea?"

"It may seem dumb to you, but, yes, I am really going through with it. OK?"

"OK. And you can talk to me about the case after dinner tonight. Now let's go inside before Mom thinks you've run away from home," Danny said. He swung at her with his knapsack and reached for the door.

A few minutes later Christine was kneeling on her bed, dangling Phiz's catnip mouse over his head. The cat batted at it lazily.

"What do you do all day when I'm at school,

31

Phiz?" Chris asked him playfully. "Do you hunt mice? Go running? Take long baths?"

Phiz winked sleepily at his mistress.

She nodded. "I know. You sleep all day. You get good and rested so you can have dinner and go to bed." Christine leaned on her elbow and tickled the cat's stomach. "What a hard life you lead."

She stood up and started unpacking her book bag, piling the books up on her desk, which was really a door, supported by a pair of sawhorses.

"Geology. Bluh." She threw her earth science book down. "American history. Another bluh." That book joined the first one. "Trig. Mrs. Feinbaum, what a witch," she murmured. She dug around in the bag and pulled out another book. "Social studies. Ugh." Then she pulled out the last book in the bag. "Shakespeare." She paused and looked at the paperback in her hand, turning back to Phiz.

"Now this, Phizball, is great. We're reading *Macbeth* and if there ever was a great mystery, this is it." She could have sworn Phiz's ears perked up. So she continued. "See, the Macbeths kill King Duncan, so that's not the mystery, but they're so afraid someone will find out they end up killing more people, and Lady

32

Macbeth goes crazy, and they're all these prophecies. Great crime," Christine said and sighed. "It's wonderful."

She rolled Phiz around on the bed. "And, as you know, I began work today on the Gym Equipment Heist. I don't want to bore you, but I did meet a great witness—at least he's really cute and funny. I think you'd like him."

Christine paused again as her thoughts returned to that afternoon's events. . . .

"And we hit it off right away—he seems to think as I do, know what I mean? I'd better question him further. I wouldn't mind having an excuse to talk to him again."

The sound of the Harters' front door opening and closing brought Christine back to the present. Her father was home, and that meant it was dinner time. She rolled off the bed and ran downstairs to join her family.

Christine waited for her chance to talk with Danny. It came right after the main course.

She stood up and started clearing the table.

"Why don't you help," Mrs. Harter asked Danny. She used her no-nonsense tone that meant he didn't have a choice.

Danny and Christine jostled each other going through the door to the kitchen.

"Hey, watch it you big oaf," Christine said half seriously.

Their mother called from the dining room. "There's new ice cream, Danny."

"Where?" he answered, stacking dishes.

Christine groaned. "In the oven, you dope. Where else? I'll get it. You get the bowls."

Christine expertly scooped vanilla ice cream into bowls and then carefully dripped fudge sauce over them. She looked up at her brother. "Dan?"

He was staring intently at the ice cream. "What?"

"What does a team manager do? On a school team, not a professional team," she added.

"Oh, you mean like Andy? I saw you talking to him this afternoon. What was all that about, anyway?"

Christine remembered exactly how they had smiled at each other. "Nothing. Just tell me what he does."

"Well, he sort of makes sure everything gets done."

Christine glanced at him, adding whipped cream and nuts to each bowl of ice cream. "That's it? That's all you can say? What does he do to make sure everything gets done?"

Danny grabbed one of the bowls. Christine

handed him a spoon and he attacked his dessert. After he swallowed a few mouthfuls, he said, "Everything. He makes sure arrangements for away games are set, he helps the coach with the statistics. He keeps track of equipment and uniforms. Satisfied?"

Christine nodded thoughtfully. She picked up the two sundaes for her parents and headed back to the dining room. "Bring mine in, will you?" she called to Danny.

"Hey, wait a minute. I almost forgot." Danny's excited tone made Christine stop.

"Go on, tell me," she urged him.

Danny smiled smugly. "I know something about this case you don't know yet."

Christine walked back to where her brother stood, licking fudge sauce off the back of his spoon. "What?" she asked.

Danny raised an eyebrow. "Excuse me?"

"Danny, if you don't cut it out right now, I'll tell embarrassing secrets about you to your football team."

Dan put his empty bowl in the sink. "OK, OK," he said. His teasing tone disappeared as he said, "Something else was stolen from the gym today. A very expensive stopwatch."

Christine felt a sickening thump in her chest. If anyone had seen her sneaking into the locker room, he'd think that she was the thief—just as Andy had assumed she was that afternoon. But she also felt angry because of the look of disappointment and sadness on her brother's face. She knew he was thinking that the thief had to be someone on his team, one of his buddies. Whoever was stealing was taking more than objects—he was stealing the team's spirit and trust they had in one another.

"Any ideas? Did you notice who left the field during practice?" she asked.

Danny shook his head mournfully. "I didn't. When you're practicing you don't really notice anything. The coach left, I guess. And Andy. But anyone else could have." He held his hands up in a gesture of despair. "I just don't know."

Christine looked up at her brother and put her hand on his arm. "Dan? I'm sorry this is happening. I know it's a drag to have someone stealing from the team. But I'm going to find out who did it, I promise."

Danny shrugged. "Right," he said gruffly.

"Say," Christine continued, wanting to change the subject, "What do you think of Teri Hutchinson? You know her—she's on the JV cheerleading squad."

"Yeah. I know her. What I think of her is none of your business," Danny responded.

Christine picked up the two bowls again and said, "Don't get all hyper. I'm just doing a little research. Now would you bring my ice cream in, please?" she turned to go into the dining room.

"Chris, that's lovely!" Mrs. Harter beamed at her daughter as the two returned. "But a bit on the melted side, wouldn't you say?"

"Hmmm." Christine toyed with her ice cream. She was thinking about how evasive Andy had been. *"He keeps track of equipment,"* she remembered Danny saying. She felt apprehensive about the case. Suddenly her appetite for the ice cream was gone. She wanted only to go back up to her room, review her notes, and think.

"Can I be excused, please?" Christine asked.

"Can I have her ice cream?" Danny cut in quickly.

"Yes, and yes," Mrs. Harter replied as Christine hurriedly got up from the table.

Christine ran lightly up the steps and into her room. She pulled her notepad from her back pocket, and then flopped down on her bed to read.

Q. Do you have any idea who's taking the stuff?

A. Uh—No. No, I don't. (Witness appears nervous at this question.)

Q. Did anyone leave the field during practice? . . .

A. ---------------------------

The answer was a blank; Christine remembered that Andy had said, very unconvincingly, that he couldn't remember whether anyone had left—and then had changed the subject by telling her that the team was about to return.

She closed the notepad and pulled thoughtfully at a lock of hair. In her mind she saw Andy's smiling, handsome face. He'd quit smiling, when she had asked him those questions. She looked at Phiz who was still curled up next to her stuffed animals.

Christine walked to her bookcase and ran her forefinger over the spines. She read off titles: "*A Case of Masks, The Jabberwocky Murders, The Blind Witness, Love or Murder, Mr. Adair's Decision, The Sound of Breaking Glass.*" She pulled out the last book, turned, and leaned against the bookcase, flipping through the pages of the well-thumbed paperback.

"In all of these stories the detective questioned a suspect who appeared to be honest and well liked. And then turned out to be the murderer," she told Phiz.

Of course, Christine knew that stealing equipment wasn't exactly murder. What the crime was made no difference to her. In her mind, criminals usually acted in the same way.

"In fact," she mused, "the murderer is quite often a really popular guy. Everyone knows that's true. It's Harter's First Law of Crime." She put the book down as she read from her notepad again, " 'The person everyone likes most is the criminal. And Harter's Second Law of Crime is: The person everyone says could never have done it did it. Someone everyone likes.' " She glanced at the sleeping cat as she flipped the pad shut. "So, I need someone with access to the equipment, someone with a motive, and someone who fits Harter's First and Second Laws of Crime."

Christine was suddenly very tired. She didn't like the conclusion she had just reached. She shook her head as she carefully placed *The Sound of Breaking Glass* back on the shelf. "It would have to be someone like Andy Mellon."

Chapter Four

"People, homework to the front, please," Mrs. Feinbaum said. She vigorously erased fifty minutes worth of illegible chalk marks from the board.

Christine slumped down a bit farther in her seat, guiltily looking around her. She had spent the night before chewing on her pencil and staring into space. She had only finished half the problems. Christine grabbed the sheaf of papers from the boy who sat behind her, and placed her paper on the bottom of the stack before passing it forward.

The last bell of the day sounded, and the members of Mrs. Feinbaum's trigonometry class pushed toward the door. Christine was at the head of the group.

Teri Hutchinson caught up with Christine at their adjoining lockers.

"That woman is such a bore," Teri said. She took an apple out of her locker and began munching hungrily.

"What's with you?" Christine asked, amazed at her friend's voracious appetite. "Just released from prison camp or something?"

Teri laughed. "With Mrs. Feinbaum, just about. No, I skipped lunch, and I'm starving. I'm afraid I'll pass out at practice."

"Oh, so you thought you'd fill up on a hearty meal of one apple. Right?" Christine asked.

Teri smiled sheepishly. Then she said, "Come on. You know perfectly well I'm on a diet." She looked enviously at Christine's slim figure. "Some of us were blessed with perfect figures, and some of us were blessed with the ability to diet."

"Well, I think it's pretty dumb. You look fine to me."

"Thanks," Teri said.

The two rummaged in their lockers for a moment. Christine tried to remember all her homework assignments; she wanted to get everything together as fast as she could so she'd be able to work on the case. Teri slammed her locker shut and swung a pink duffel bag over her shoulder. "Well, I've got to get down to practice. We've got a game against Hawthorne on Saturday, and the cheerleaders from there are perfect. Bye!"

Christine watched as Teri joined some girls down the hall and headed for the gym. She liked all the JV cheerleaders and had considered trying out for the squad the past year. She'd even gone to tryout practices. But on the day she was supposed to have performed for the judges, she'd started a new mystery in study hall. Christine had been so absorbed in the book that she missed tryouts altogether.

She closed her locker, deep in thought.

Christine jogged across campus, her books bouncing by her side. By the time she had passed through the parking lot and reached the football field she was slightly out of breath. She didn't have a very clear idea of what she should do once she got there. If anyone asked, she was ready to tell them she was there to watch her brother practice. It sounded dumb, but it was better than announcing to the world that she was tracking the thief. After the teasing she'd gotten the day before, from Andy and her brother, Christine had decided not to tell anyone else she was a detective.

The sound of agonized yells and grunts reached her ears as she approached, and she saw about fifteen boys running into padded metal posts, pushing them backward four or five feet each time. *Is this what they do?* she wondered. Another fifteen boys were running through a series of tires, and off on the sidelines, she could see Andy Mellon taking footballs out of a huge bag.

Suddenly embarrassed, Christine scanned the field, searching for some kind of cover. But there was none. Deciding to take the bold approach, she climbed to the top of the bleachers and opened her book bag. She pretended to be absorbed in her book as she heard someone coming up the bleachers toward her.

"Hi, Christine. Can't keep away from the football team, huh?" Andy called, bounding up to her.

Christine blushed. "Are you kidding? I'm just trying to keep what tan I have left from the summer. The football field just happens to be the best place for sunning, that's all," she said casually.

Andy sat down beside her and leaned back, his elbows on the next tier. "No, really. Are you still hot on the trail of our infamous football thief?" he asked, smiling up at her.

The autumn sunlight glinted on his brown hair and made his keen blue eyes sparkle. Christine found herself smiling in spite of herself; but then she remembered that all the evidence was against Andy, and she turned away, frowning.

Andy didn't seem to notice her change in attitude. "I guess you know what happened yesterday afternoon, right? Did Danny tell you?" he inquired.

She nodded.

"And that was one valuable watch. It was one of those expensive German models that you can't even buy over here." He whistled softly. "Whoever it is, he must need the money pretty badly. I know what it's like to be broke."

Stunned, Christine turned toward him, scarcely knowing what to say. If he was the thief, how could he talk about it? What a cool customer!

"Oh, really?" she managed to choke out.

"Sure," he said. "My folks are pretty hard up right now. I've got two little brothers, so my mom can't work, and two months ago my dad got laid off . . ." Andy's voice trailed off, and he sat staring ahead into space.

Christine couldn't help herself. She felt a rush of affection and sympathy for him. It was terrible to think of anyone her age worrying about the things that Christine left to her parents.

She laid her hand on his arm. "I'm sorry, Andy."

He looked over at her and then down at the small hand on his sleeve. She quickly took it away.

"No, I'm sorry," he said quickly. "I shouldn't have said anything. Most people—I don't know." He smiled at her wistfully. "I can talk to you, can't I, Christine?"

Christine nodded again.

Andy continued to talk to her, almost dreamily, as he gazed out across the field. "Anyway, my dad does pick up part-time jobs here and there. He's real handy—so am I, I guess, but there's no real security in it. They do have my college savings, though, so we'll make it."

"Oh, Andy, no!" Christine thought her heart would break for him. "Will you have to give up going to college?"

He shrugged. "I don't know. I'll probably have to quit the team and get a job after school. But my folks said not yet." He stopped speaking and looked out across the field again.

Christine shifted uncomfortably. There was nothing she could do to help Andy, except listen. She turned to him, and her hand hit her book bag. It fell over on the bleacher, and her trig book slid out. She caught it just before it slid through to the ground.

Andy glanced at it and recognized it, smiling. "I bet you have Mrs. Feinbaum, right?"

Christine smiled back at him. "Do I ever—I have her about five times a week more than I can stand."

"Don't be so hard on her. I think she's trying as hard as she can."

Christine was amazed by Andy's compassion. "Are you serious?"

Andy nodded and took the book from her hand. Opening the cover, he read the names of the other students who had the book before her. "Look at this. Eric Munsen. He was in my class. And he almost always fell asleep." He smiled at her again. "So you can be sure the book is in good condition—he never used it."

Christine found herself drawn to Andy. *He's a suspect*, she reminded herself. She wanted to believe Andy was innocent, but he did have a powerful motive—he needed the money. Christine forced herself to get back to the case.

"By the way," she began, looking straight ahead. "Where was that watch taken from, anyway?"

"Still hard at work, huh?" Andy smiled. "It was in the cage the last time I saw it."

"I see," she said calmly. When she had been hiding behind the box of basketballs, she had seen Andy pick up a small box and look suspiciously around him.

His next words surprised her even more. "I don't suppose anything fell into your pocket while you were sneaking around the locker room yesterday?" He said it casually.

"What? Are you crazy? I'm a detective, I don't steal things! What kind of a person do you think I am?" she demanded. She was shocked that he could even think such a thing.

"Sorry—I was just joking," Andy said.

Andy's dazzling smile disarmed Christine once again, and her anger passed. "Well, OK. If you *were* just joking," she remarked.

He punched her knee playfully. "Of course I was, Christine." He glanced at his watch. "Look—I've got to get back to work. A team manager isn't supposed to sit around talking to a beautiful girl all day. Even though it's more fun."

He jumped up and jogged back down the bleachers, leaving Christine smiling to herself. She gathered her books together in a daze and made her way down to the ground.

She decided to walk home instead of waiting another hour for her brother. She was suddenly mad at herself. *You dope, how could you let him distract you so much? Andy Mellon is the prime suspect. As a matter of fact, he's the only suspect you've got and you sit there letting him question you? What a lousy, miserable, unprofessional detective you are, Christine Harter.*

Christine felt torn. Andy could be the thief. But she couldn't get those words "beautiful girl" out of her head. Could he actually like her? It was so confusing.

She kicked angrily at a stone in her path and jumped nervously when a car honked at her as it passed. A familiar green station wagon pulled up just ahead of her, and as she ran up to it, her mother called, "How about a lift?"

"Hi, Mom," Christine said as she climbed into the car.

"Hello, sweetheart," Mrs. Harter said. She leaned over to kiss her daughter on the forehead. "You look like you're running away from school."

Christine smiled and leaned against the door. "Where are you coming from, anyway? The grocery store?

Her mother turned to her with mock surprise. "You *are* a brilliant detective! How on earth did you ever figure out where I've been?"

"The four bags of chow in the backseat of this jalopy gave your dirty secret away, lady. The jig's up," Christine said, jabbing her thumb over one shoulder.

Mrs. Harter nodded, turning her attention back to the traffic. "There are some cookies at the top of one of those bags, I believe, which you may open as a reward."

Christine pulled a package of Oreos out of a bag, and opened them. As she pulled out a cookie, she said, "Mom, how do you ever know if someone is dishonest? I mean, if you don't have any real proof."

"Well, that's pretty complex, dear. But I think I know what you mean." She paused, then said, "Unless you have proof that someone lied or cheated, you don't know for sure. And the sad thing is you may never know for sure. But as much as possible, Christine, you have to trust your instincts."

Christine shrugged. "But I don't have a lot of confidence in my instincts. If I had your instincts I probably would, though," she added, smiling at her mom.

"Thank you, dear. That's a nice compliment. But, really, like our philosophy of criminal justice, you're assumed innocent until proven guilty. So if you feel in your heart that someone is honest, and nothing happens to change that view, then you must assume that he is an honest person. After all, it isn't necessary for people to go around proving themselves in our society. We should just take it for granted." She looked thoughtfully over at her daughter. "Why all the soul-searching?"

Christine sighed heavily. "It's this case. It's making me think twice about things I once took for granted."

Her mother glanced at her, obviously surprised. "This case? Are you following through with the thefts at school?"

"Oh, Mom, don't tell me you're shocked, too! Everyone keeps saying, 'You're not really trying to solve this case, are you?' I'm sick of it." Christine stared sullenly out the window.

"Who said anything about being shocked?"

her mother said, her voice low. "I'm very proud of you. But I hope you aren't disappointed if nothing comes of it all."

"No, Mom. I won't be disappointed, believe me." *Believe me, there won't be any reason for disappointment. I'm going to solve this case*, she thought, her face grim.

They pulled into the driveway. Christine helped her mother put away the groceries. Then she went to her room. "Phiz?" she called. Her cat was nowhere to be found. "OK, Speckler, Rondo. I've got to talk to you," she said. But for the first time in her life, she felt foolish talking out loud to her stuffed animals.

"Sorry, guys," she said, smoothing Rondo's silky whiskers. "I think I need someone a bit more intelligent to talk to. I'll see you later."

She wandered into the bathroom and absently started brushing her hair. The harder she brushed, the angrier she felt. Finally she put down the brush and looked at herself in the mirror.

"You! You are such a poor substitute for a criminal investigator. Don't you know how to interrogate a suspect? Don't you know the first thing about maintaining your cover? What happened to that razor-sharp mind of yours? What about the brilliant work you did on all those other cases in books?"

She stopped. The memory of the sun on Andy's hair filled her thoughts. She looked up again at her reflection. "He couldn't be doing it. He's too nice." She broke off. "Andy can't be a thief. He just doesn't seem like a criminal." Christine looked down as Phiz appeared and began weaving himself in and out between her ankles. She looked back at her reflection and moaned, "Oh, Phiz! This is going to be a lot harder than I thought."

Chapter Five

"Hamburger please," Christine said to Joe, the man behind the counter in the cafeteria.

"I'll have the same. But make it two," Andy Mellon said.

Christine turned around to see him standing behind her in line and felt an unexpected rush of pleasure at finding him there.

He smiled at her. "I think you have good taste. If you think a hamburger is the way to go, I wouldn't dream of doing anything else," he said.

Blushing, Christine pushed her tray along the rails. She grabbed a bowl of pudding and a carton of milk, then fumbled in her pocket for her money. She was worried that Andy would want to sit with her, and more worried that he wouldn't.

She stared straight ahead as she made her way to her table, a small round one in a corner by the windows. Usually Christine liked to sit there by herself and read during lunch. But even as she unloaded her tray, she hoped Andy would join her.

"Can I sit with you?" Andy asked.

She hardly dared look up. "I usually read during lunch," she mumbled, suddenly afraid of having him next to her. *Keep a professional perspective*, she warned herself.

She glanced up. Andy was wearing khakis and a blue shirt that set off the sparkling blue of his eyes. To Christine he appeared anything but criminal.

He smiled. "You read every day Christine; I want to talk to you about the case."

Her resolve crumbled. She wanted to eat lunch with him. Christine nodded, and Andy sat down. "I've read this one a million times anyway," Christine remarked. She tossed the paperback she was reading next to her plate.

"Can I see it?" Andy asked, picking it up. " '*Longwood Castle.* Spine-tingling suspense,' " he read from the back cover. Andy raised his eyebrows. "What's this about, anyway?"

Christine said, "This woman, Portia, gets married to this guy, Andre Damian, and she's really crazy about him. Then all this really weird stuff happens, and she thinks someone's trying to kill her. She begins to wonder if her husband is responsible. She has to figure it all out."

"And did he do it?" Andy asked, taking a bite of his hamburger.

Christine swallowed a bite. She paused. "It was the uncle. I knew by chapter eight the first time I read it," she said.

Andy smiled. "No kidding? Do you always figure it out before the end? By the way," he added, pretending to be disappointed. "You've spoiled the ending for me."

Christine smiled at him for the first time that day. "You wouldn't have read it anyway," she said. She slipped the book back into her bag.

"No, actually, I'm more interested in watching you solve a real-life mystery," Andy said. "I've been trying to do a little detecting on my own, but it's tough when I've got to be on the field most of the time while the robberies take place. I'd like to work with you to help you catch the guy who's stealing from the team. I want him nailed."

"You do?" Christine asked, incredulous. "Why?"

He seemed surprised. "Why? Why else? I want the thefts stopped. They're undermining team spirit."

Christine realized that she had almost let him see that she suspected him. But if he was guilty, why would he want to team up with her? Was he planning to lead her on a wild goose chase or something? Still, she reasoned, it would give her a good excuse to watch him.

There was another little voice in her that was saying, *And you'll get to spend a lot of time with him, too. He's asking to be with you to work on a serious project.* Christine tried to dismiss that idea. It was keeping her from being a serious detective.

She drew a deep breath. "I could use some help," she said, then added, "I need someone to look around in the boys' locker room for me."

Her new partner raised an eyebrow. "That's the sort of stuff you'd never do, right?" he asked, looking her in the eye.

"Right," she said. They both laughed.

Still staring into Christine's eyes, Andy said

softly, "I think I'm going to enjoy working with you, Christine."

The noise of the cafeteria surrounded them. Christine finished her lunch hurriedly. She wiped her hands on a napkin and tried to appear as businesslike as possible. She was almost afraid that her voice might give her away. "OK, what do you say we meet on the bleachers during practice and talk over what we've both come up with so far?" she asked.

Andy picked up his second burger as Christine stood up. "Sure thing, boss. By the way, it's OK with me if you're sort of in charge of the investigation."

"Oh, really? How very generous of you," Christine said sarcastically.

Startled, Andy looked up at her and immediately said, "I'm sorry. I didn't mean it to sound that way. Honest."

She shrugged, hiding a smile of her own. "No problem. See you later." She swung her book bag over her shoulder and left him there.

Christine wove her way around the tables in the crowded lunchroom. She was in emotional turmoil. All of the evidence seemed to point to Andy, but she just couldn't believe him capable of stealing from his own team—

from anyone, in fact. And she really liked him, liked being with him and talking to him.

Christine spent the rest of the day struggling to keep her attention on her schoolwork. Mrs. Feinbaum was especially boring in trig class, and it took all Christine's self-discipline to keep her eyes on the board and not in her case notebook.

But the last bell finally sounded, and Christine rushed out to the football field. She wasn't sure if her enthusiasm was because she would be seeing Andy or because she was working on the case. She was early and sat alone on the bleachers, savoring the golden, autumn sunshine. *It doesn't matter why I'm happy,* Christine thought. *I just am.*

The sound of approaching voices and laughter brought her back to the football field, and Christine watched as the team members jogged out to it. She spotted her brother among the players. He waved to her as he snapped his chin guard in place.

"Hey, Chris! You're here again? Going to join the team?" Danny shouted.

She smiled, shaking her head. She watched the team warm up for a few minutes. Out of the corner of her eye she glimpsed two lone figures walking toward the field. She recognized

Andy and Coach Keeler. They were deep in conversation; Andy was gesturing with his hands, and the coach was shaking his head. When they reached the bleachers, Christine heard Andy say, "I'll just be a minute, coach." And he turned toward her with a wave.

She watched him run lightly up the bleachers to the top tier where she sat, and found herself smiling in anticipation of talking to him again.

"What was all that about?" Christine asked him, nodding her head in the direction of Coach Keeler.

Andy waved his hand dismissively. "Nothing. Coach and I don't see eye to eye on everything."

"Meaning that usually you do?" Christine asked, curious.

He nodded. "Yeah, actually, we do. He's a great guy. I'm sorry Coach Buzzeo got sick this fall, but I'm glad we've got Coach Keeler. He's a lot more modern than Buzzeo."

"Give me an example," Christine said encouragingly.

Andy thought for a moment. "Well, he's always talking about psychology. Sports psychology. It's really interesting. He minored in psychology in college, and he applies it to

61

everything. For example, he says you've got to understand the mentality of the person who's stealing equipment, in order to catch him," Andy said.

Christine nodded. "I know what he's talking about. That's the only way to solve a mystery."

Andy stared across the field to where the coach stood, shouting out drills. "He's real friendly," Andy said. "I mean, right from the beginning of the season, he was always asking me about how I was doing in school, and how my family is. Things like that really make a difference. He cares." He looked back at Christine. "Know what I mean?"

She smiled. "Yeah. I know what you mean." She looked across at Keeler, too. "How is Buzzeo doing? He had a stroke, right?"

"Yeah. Nothing serious. I mean, he wasn't paralyzed, or anything like that," Andy said. "But he's got to be careful for a few months."

"My grandfather had a stroke, once, a long time ago," Christine said. "That's when I started reading mysteries, actually. The hospital was pretty far away, and I needed something to read in the car and in the waiting rooms and stuff."

Andy asked quietly, "How old were you?"

Christine smiled. "Ten. I guess it wasn't so

long ago. But I got hooked. At first I could never figure them out. When the murderer was revealed, I was always surprised. In fact, it amazed me so much that I decided that I wanted to be able to solve them. I can even remember when I first decided I was going to be a detective."

"Yeah? When?" he asked.

"On Christmas Day, three years ago. I had received a whole bunch of detective stories, and I spent all day reading them. It was *The Barefoot Thief* that made up my mind. Ever since then, I've wanted to be a detective."

"Wow," Andy said, shaking his head. "I really admire that. Most people never know what they want. You've known for three years already, and you're only in high school."

"Well, some people think it's a really dumb idea," she said, pushing a curl behind her ear.

"I bet the people who think it's a dumb idea don't know what they want to do themselves," Andy commented. "They're probably jealous of you because you've figured out your life already."

"You know, I never thought of that," she said. "Sometimes I worry that maybe I shouldn't be a detective since everyone thinks it's so crazy."

"Well, quit worrying," Andy said firmly.

Christine held out her hand. "Thanks, Andy." They shook hands, grinning at each other.

Andy shrugged his shoulders. "Glad to help out."

They were still holding hands, so Christine gently pulled her hand away. But Andy held on.

"There's a home game tomorrow, and I don't really have to do much during games. Will you sit with me?" Andy asked.

Christine was afraid—afraid to get more involved with Andy. She had so many doubts about him. But she wanted to say yes.

"Sure. I'd like to," she said. He let go of her hand.

"Good. Can you meet me here at eleven-thirty? I'm sorry I can't pick you up. There's stuff I have to do before the game starts. Then I'm free, and we can watch together," Andy said. He stood up as he spoke.

"No, I don't mind at all," Christine said.

"Great. I've got to go now or Keeler is going to get another team manager." He turned to walk down the bleachers, then faced her again. "We never got around to talking about the case, partner," he said.

Christine shrugged her shoulders. "I guess we'll have to have a conference tomorrow, then."

Andy laughed and bounded down to the field.

For the next hour Christine sat in the warm sunlight and watched football practice. Other students drifted by, watched for a while, and left, and one faculty member came out to speak to Coach Keeler. But no one on the team ever left the field.

Then, with a start, Christine realized that Andy was jogging toward the gym by himself. A quick glance at her watch told her that there was still half an hour to go before the end of practice, and she was instantly on the alert. She waited for Andy to return.

The minutes ticked by slowly. Twenty minutes after he had left the field, Andy returned to the practice area. She tried to catch his eye, but he didn't look in her direction.

"Christine!" Danny shouted.

She looked over at him and waved.

"Stay there," he yelled. "I'll be ready in ten minutes."

Danny and the rest of his team jogged tiredly toward the gym, leaving Christine alone on the football field. She huddled in her jacket, suddenly cold. A few clouds had covered the sun, and the October air turned chilly.

As the temperature dropped, so did Christine's spirits. She tried to recapture her previous happiness, but she couldn't. She sat there, suddenly downcast.

As she glanced again at her watch, she realized that twenty minutes had passed. Where was Danny? He was hardly ever late.

She looked quickly over toward the gym in time to see Danny come outside and wave impatiently at her. As she gathered up her books, he got into his car in the parking lot.

She began to run to the car because he was honking the horn.

"What's wrong with you?" she demanded breathlessly as she scrambled in beside him.

Danny's face was rigid with anger.

"What *is* it?" Christine asked.

He looked at her grimly as he backed out of the parking space. "Eleven watches. Eight class rings. Right out of the locked drawer in the coach's office!"

Angrily he held out his wrist; Christine could see that his watch was gone. "If this doesn't stop, there won't be anything left for that creep to steal," Danny muttered.

Christine suddenly understood her mood change. She'd seen Andy leave the field, alone. More things had been stolen. She'd been afraid that this would happen.

Christine couldn't deny it any longer. Andy was the thief, and she had to stop him.

Chapter Six

Christine woke up early on Saturday morning, barely rested from a night spent tossing and turning. There was now no question in her mind. Andy Mellon had to be the thief.

Andy's family needed money. Maybe he'd just wanted to help out at home. *But*, Christine thought, *that's no excuse. He could get a job.* And he was responsible for all the equipment. That meant he had easy access to it. He was the only team member to leave the field the day before, Christine was sure of that. She had gone over all of their conversations. Andy had acted suspiciously. The case was solved.

Instead of feeling happy that she had solved her first real case, Christine felt awful. She lay glumly in bed, her pajamas twisted around her body. Irritably, she tried to untwist them and heard them rip. She closed her eyes in defeat. "I feel like throwing up," she said out loud.

Phiz jumped on the bed and curled up beside her, immediately beginning to purr. But when she did not respond immediately by rubbing his neck, his tail began to twitch.

"Phiz, you are an impatient pain in the neck," Christine snapped.

Phiz squinted slightly and then yawned in her face. Arching his back, he jumped down and stalked huffily out the door.

Christine followed him out and made her way to the bathroom. She stopped short at the closed door and knocked lightly.

"Dan—nee! Hurry up in there!"

She heard him answer, but she couldn't tell what he'd said. At least he knew she was waiting.

Christine started downstairs and slipped. She landed hard on her ankle and shrieked in pain. Then she burst into tears.

"Honey, honey, what's wrong?" Mr. Harter said, rushing into the hall from the den, an envelope in one hand and his coffee in the other. He set them down and tried to help his daughter to her feet. Phiz's mangled catnip mouse lay just in front of her.

"I—I twisted my ankle! I can't stand." she gasped out.

Mrs. Harter came into the hall and knelt in front of Christine. She tenderly pulled the injured foot toward her.

"Does that hurt, dear?" she asked, looking intently into Christine's tear-stained face.

Christine had just realized that the pain, at first sharp, was going away. But she still couldn't stop crying and didn't know how to justify it. So she nodded meekly.

Mrs. Harter stood up, turning to her husband. "Frank, help me get her back upstairs."

"Shouldn't we take her to the hospital?" he asked, an anxious frown on his face.

Christine's heart sank, and she managed to gulp down the last of her tears. "No! No, I'm OK, really," she said.

Her mother nodded. "Well, let's just see if we can get you back to bed anyway. I think Chris and I can manage if you'd go make her some hot cocoa, dear," she said to her husband. She turned back to Christine and put one arm around her. "Now up you go."

The two hobbled upstairs, and Christine feigned a limp. When she was finally back in

71

her bed her mother sat down beside her, putting a cool hand on her forehead.

"Now what's all the crying about?"

"My ankle—"

Mrs. Harter shook her head. "You never cry when you hurt yourself. Your ankle isn't swollen or red, and you didn't flinch when I touched it, so it couldn't possibly hurt enough to make you cry. Am I right?" she asked.

Christine flushed.

"Now do you want to tell me what's wrong?"

"I don't know, Mom. I just feel—I don't know." Christine sat back and looked gloomily out the window.

"Here's the cocoa," Mr. Harter said, hurrying into the room. "How are you?"

"I'm OK, Dad. It just hurts a little. Thanks for the cocoa."

"Hey, what's with the invalid routine?" Danny stopped outside the door.

"Don't you have a game to get ready for?" Mr. Harter asked soberly.

Danny grinned. "Against Hawthorne. We've got to beat 'em."

Christine felt as if she'd just been kicked in the stomach. The game! She was supposed to meet Andy at the game! But she couldn't. She knew she couldn't. She started to get out of

72

bed, forgetting that she was supposed to be injured.

"Whoa! Where do you think you're going, young lady?" her father asked.

She bit her lip. "I—I've got to make a phone call."

Her mother looked at her skeptically, a wry smile on her face. "Can't it wait, Chris?"

Christine looked at her parents. She felt so stupid to have made such a fuss about her ankle. Her mother knew she was faking it, but seemed to be going along with it in front of her dad and brother. She looked at her father. "I was supposed to meet someone at the football game. And—now I can't go because of my ankle."

"Well, honey, your mom can make the call for you. I think you should stay in bed and rest that foot."

"No! I mean, I can hop into your room and use the phone there. Then I'll get right back in bed and stay here all day. Promise," Christine said.

"All right, Chris," Mrs. Harter said. She watched her daughter thoughtfully.

Once Christine was in the hall, she ran on tiptoe to her parents' room to use the phone.

She flipped impatiently through the phone

73

book. "Melius, Mellan, Mellan, Mellon. Here." She dialed the number anxiously. She was dreading the conversation with Andy.

"Hello?" A woman answered the phone. Chris could hear a child crying in the background.

"Hello. Can I speak to Andy, please? This is Christine Harter."

A moment passed before Andy's voice came on the line. "Hi, Christine. I was just thinking about you. What's up?"

Suddenly Christine was at a loss for words. She knew she had to cancel her date with him, but a part of her held back. "Andy, I can't come to the game today," she finally said.

There was a brief silence. "Why?" he asked, sounding distant.

"I—I sprained my ankle," Christine said. She hated using that as an excuse.

"Oh, no! Are you all right?" Andy was clearly concerned.

"No. I mean, yes," Christine said. "I just have to stay in bed all day, that's all."

"How about if I stop by after the game?" he offered.

"No!" she said loudly. "Don't do that! I'll be sleeping all day," she finished lamely.

"Well, I'll call you later, OK?" he asked in a flat voice.

"Sure. Sorry, Andy," Christine said.

She hung up the phone and sat staring at it for a moment. Then she limped back dramatically to her bedroom, but there was no one there to notice. She climbed back into bed and reached for the steaming mug of cocoa.

Even though she had hardly slept the night before, she felt alert and energetic. She didn't like the idea of spending the day in bed because of her "twisted ankle." She settled into the pillows and sipped at the chocolate.

She still liked Andy. She might even be in love with him. He was easy to talk to, fun to be with, extremely attractive, and funny. *And he's a lying, dishonest person who steals from his own football team*, she told herself.

Christine groaned, hitting her forehead with the palm of her hand. "What am I going to do?" she wailed mournfully. "I can't turn him in. What kind of a detective does that make me?"

Christine had always thought that solving a real crime would be easy. Once you knew who the criminal was, you simply handed him over to the police. Now she wasn't so sure. Falling in love with the thief was something she had never anticipated.

But, she thought, *I don't have any proof*. She hadn't actually seen Andy take anything and hadn't found any of the stolen items in his possession. Yet she could never be happy with Andy until she knew for sure that he was innocent.

Something else bothered her also. It was obvious that Andy liked her, but if he was the thief, he could just be pretending to like her, to throw her off. To think he might be faking his attraction to her was painful. *Why did I ever make such a big deal out of my ankle? It doesn't hurt at all anymore,* she thought.

She looked around her bedroom. She was tired of thinking. She needed something to do. Christine saw her book bag and remembered that she could read *Longwood Castle*, which she had packed in her bag Friday. She got out of bed, grabbed it, and hopped back under her covers.

Although she had already read it many times, she knew that it would take her mind off her problems. She leaned back against the headboard and began to read.

* * *

At six o'clock Danny stopped by her bedroom. "You'll be glad to know we beat Hawthorne," he said. But the rest of his news sank Christine's spirits even lower. "But the thief struck again. The receipts for the whole day were stolen from Coach Keeler's office. He says that if the thief doesn't come forward within the next few days he's bringing in the police."

"Money?" Christine asked. "The thief took money?"

Danny nodded, then left to go to his room.

Christine slumped down into her pillows, a dull ache in her heart. *Oh, Andy,* she thought, *what are you doing?* She had no answers anymore. So she did the only thing she could manage at that moment—Christine cried herself to sleep.

Chapter Seven

"Christine? Did you hear me?" Mrs. Harter asked.

Christine looked up from the newspaper to find her mother peering at her. "What?" she asked.

"I've asked you three times to pass the jam," Mrs. Harter replied.

Christine blushed. "Sorry, Mom." She passed the jam and went back to staring blankly at the Sunday comics spread out before her on the breakfast table.

Christine felt strangely refreshed that morning. All her crying the night before had left her feeling cleansed. It had changed her; she knew that she could do the right thing now. She only needed evidence. When she got it, she would turn Andy in to the school authorities.

Christine looked up from her comics; she and her mother were alone at the table. Mrs. Harter was watching her with a worried look on her face. Christine was certain that her mother was about to ask her something.

Christine was right.

"How is your case coming along, Chris?" Mrs. Harter asked casually.

"Fine," Christine replied.

"Oh?"

Christine looked at her mother. She really wanted to tell her the truth. She sighed. "Actually, it's not fine."

Her mother nodded and took a sip of her coffee. "Want to tell me about it?"

"If I tell you, you've got to promise you'll let me handle it," Christine said.

Mrs. Harter looked as if she wanted to object, but pressed her lips together instead. She cupped her hands around her warm coffee mug and nodded again.

"OK. I think I know who's been taking the stuff from the gym. But—well, everyone likes this guy, and he's having a rough time at home right now. His folks are really broke. I mean, I just don't know if I should just go ahead and tell the coach who's doing it."

"Oh, Chris. You've got to. No matter who it is, he's committing crimes. There's no excuse for that, no matter how poor his family is," Mrs. Harter said.

"I know that," Christine said. "But there's more to it than that."

Her mother raised her eyebrows.

Taking a deep breath, Christine said, "I really like him, too. A lot."

Her mother sat absolutely still and silent for a few moments. Then Mrs. Harter clasped her hands together and said, "Christine, I hope you aren't making a big mistake. I'd hate to see you get hurt. In fact, I'm not sure you should continue with this business."

"But, Mom. You said you would let me handle this. And I will," Christine told her. She looked down at the paper again, trying to organize her thoughts. "Being a detective isn't what I thought it would be, but that doesn't mean I'm going to stop being one. I'm having to do a lot of thinking about me, and about—this person." She looked squarely at her mother. "But I will do the right thing. I just haven't figured out how yet."

Her mother took Christine's hand. "I'm

sorry, Christine. I think I've underestimated you. But this sounds like pretty dangerous territory emotionally. I just hope you don't end up the loser in all this."

Christine smiled ruefully and said, "This situation didn't come up in any of my books, so I'm going to have to trust my instincts, as you told me."

Mrs. Harter stood up and crossed behind her daughter. Leaning over Christine, she kissed her softly on the head. "Be careful of your heart, Christine. This person, whoever he is, has already stolen enough."

Christine nodded and went back to her room, deep in thought. Telling her mother she would do the right thing was fine, but what the right thing might be she still didn't know. She decided that doing something physical and constructive might clear her head. She started to clean her room.

She turned on the radio to her favorite station and sang along as she hung up clothes, organized her desk, and dusted off her shelves. As she bent down to pick up a sock, she found *Longwood Castle* lying face down where it had fallen.

She picked it up and sat back on the bed with it. Her mind went back to her conversation with Andy in the lunchroom on Friday, when she was telling him about the book. *'Then all this really weird stuff happens, . . . she begins to wonder if her husband is responsible.'*

'And did he do it?' Andy had asked.

'No, it was the uncle.'

The beginnings of an idea were forming in her mind, and she lowered the book slowly. In the story the uncle made it look like the husband was guilty. *What if—even though all the evidence does point to Andy—what if somebody he likes and trusts, is doing it, and is making it* look *like Andy's doing it?* she asked herself.

Christine searched frantically through her newly organized room for her case notebook. In her hurry to find it, she undid all the work she had just done. Her room looked like a tornado had just blown through it. But she finally found it and hopped back on the bed, eager to review her notes. She flipped through the pages, reading excitedly.

Daniel Harter: "The coach said we shouldn't call the police."

Teri Hutchinson: "No one's supposed to know about it. Coach Keeler told us all to keep quiet about it. Just the people who are at the gym everyday."

Note: Coach Keeler insisted that student Mellon leave the so-called 'cage' unlocked. Equipment remains accessible. . . ."

Andy Mellon: "I keep telling the coach we should change the lock. . . . But the coach won't change it . . . He said he's seen this happen before.

Christine sat back slowly. *Careful, Harter. Be sure of what you're thinking,* she told herself.

She glanced over her notes again. "But it's not impossible. It really is not impossible. Coach Keeler could be doing it himself," she said out loud.

Christine sat down at her desk. She had to sort out the dozens of thoughts that were crowding in on her brain. She took a pencil, and began to write.

1. No one really knows anything about Keeler—he's just a substitute for Buzzeo. We don't know about his past. He could easily have faked his credentials.

2. Andy said Keeler asks questions

about his family situation all the time. Is he making sure Andy needs money desperately enough to steal?

3. Keeler is keeping the robberies quiet. Has he even told the principal? Shielding himself? He is in control. He's making sure that everyone is a suspect by keeping the cage unlocked.

She nibbled thoughtfully at the end of her pencil, looking at the words she had just written. Coach Keeler was the thief. But maybe it only made sense to her. She wanted to believe that Andy was innocent—but accusing the coach of theft could get her into a lot of trouble. She still didn't have any real evidence against *anyone*.

"I'm going to have to keep a close eye on him," she muttered. She almost didn't believe her own theory. But she was willing to investigate the coach if it would clear Andy.

On Monday afternoon Christine walked purposefully out to the field after school and sat on the bottom step of the bleachers to watch practice. She smiled absently when Andy waved from across the grass; but her attention was riveted on just one man. She watched Coach Keeler carefully.

Teri sat down next to Christine. She was drinking a diet soda. "Hi," she said, breathless from practice. "A well-deserved break."

"Hi, Teri," Christine said. Her eyes were focused on Keeler.

Teri read the nutritional information on the side of the soda can.

"Serving size five point six ounces, two point eight five servings per can. Why do they do that? It's ridiculous. Who's going to measure out five point six ounces to drink?"

Christine shrugged. "It's so it works out to exactly one calorie per serving, I guess. Otherwise it would be like two-point-oh-oh-oh-one calories per serving, or something stupid like that. I don't know."

"Why don't they just change the size of the can?"

"I don't know," Christine answered, her eyes still on the coach. "All the machines hold cans that size. It's too late to change now, I guess."

Teri looked at her friend. "Hmm. It never occurred to me before why it was like that. No wonder you're such a good detective, Chris," she added playfully.

"Thanks," she said wryly. "But it's just common sense, really."

"Well, I guess I don't have too much of that," Teri said, sighing. "Otherwise why would I be killing myself every day for a bunch of guys that don't even notice me?"

Christine finally faced her friend. "Oh, yeah? Don't be too sure of yourself, Teri. You never know who's watching you." She turned back to the field. "You never know who's watching you," she whispered, staring hard at Keeler.

"What?"

Forcing a smile, Christine stood up. "Just talking to myself. Hey, I need to ask the coach a question. Catch you later, OK?"

Teri shrugged and smoothed her ponytail. "Sure. I've got to get back to practice anyway."

The sun was warm on her back as Christine walked around the outer perimeter of the football field. It seemed as if an endless stream of boys ran past her. She saw Andy nod to the coach and head for the gym. When she walked up to Keeler, he was standing alone. His eyes were on his players.

"Hi, coach." Christine smiled. "I'm Dan Harter's sister, Christine."

He returned her smile. "Well, I'm glad to meet you, Christine. I've seen you come out to watch the team. Your brother's a great player. Glad to have him with us. OK! Ten laps! Let's go!" he shouted to his team.

Christine was startled by his sudden shift from her to the team. Then he turned and beamed at her.

The coach was still deeply tanned, and he was handsome.

She smiled even more widely. "I love to watch football, even though I don't understand any of it. I guess I'm too dumb to follow all the downs and lines of scrimmage and stuff." She shrugged, still smiling broadly and waving vaguely at the boys streaming past them. "It's totally beyond me. I just like to watch the guys."

Keeler smiled at her again, obviously pleased by Christine's ingratiating manner. "Well, I don't blame you," he said. It's a fairly complicated sport. There aren't any girls' football teams, are there?" he asked smugly.

Christine felt herself grow furious at his attitude, but she forced herself to remain cheerful—and dumb—on the outside. She had to look away for a moment to regain her composure. Andy had returned and was talking to some of the players.

"There's Andy. Poor guy, I hear his family is really broke."

The coach nodded and leaned toward Christine. "You're right. Andy cares a lot about his folks. I just hope he never does anything—foolish," he said in a secretive tone.

Christine turned an innocent gaze on the coach. "What do you mean?"

He shrugged. "Oh—nothing, I guess. But these thefts have made me—never mind," he said. To Christine, his words seemed too careful—as if he'd rehearsed them.

A few days before the coach's words might have confirmed Christine's worst fears about Andy. Now she thought he could be trying to throw suspicion on Andy. She drew a deep breath and watched the players. She wanted to ask him another question. Then her glance fell down to Keeler's feet, where his gym bag was lying open.

"Wow, that's an awesome stopwatch," she said, pulling a high-tech timepiece from the bag. She saw the name Braun inscribed on the face before Keeler grabbed it from her.

"Hey! Give me that!" he snapped angrily. He

snatched it from her and stuffed it in his pocket.

Christine turned wide eyes on the coach. "I'm sorry. Is it special or something?"

He drew a deep breath. "It's just valuable. And—and very sensitive. I'd hate to see it damaged." His earlier friendliness was gone. His tone was harsh.

"Sorry, coach, really," Christine said sweetly.

"Sure. Now look. I can't spend any more time talking to you. I've got to concentrate on some plays here, so you'll have to excuse me." Keeler zipped up his bag abruptly. Then he stalked away.

Christine stood for a moment where she was on the sideline, staring after the retreating figure. "Valuable, eh? I bet," she muttered.

Christine made a rough sketch, from memory, of the stopwatch in her notepad and wrote down the maker's name. If her hunch was right, it would be the same brand as the expensive watch that was stolen from the gym.

Would that prove anything? Christine wondered. She still wouldn't be able to turn the coach in. She made a wry face, irritated by the possibility that she could be so close, yet so far from solving the case!

But proof or not, she knew the truth at last. Andy wasn't a thief. Andy was innocent.

Chapter Eight

Christine shut the front door of her house and stood for a moment, listening. She had taken the late bus instead of waiting for Dan, so he was still at practice. The house was utterly still. Her mother's car hadn't been in the garage. Christine was alone.

She felt like a balloon, ready to explode. Andy was being framed by the real thief, Coach Keeler.

Christine hugged herself, happiness sweeping over her. All at once she had more energy than could be contained within her small room. She was excited—and frightened. She jumped up, ran downstairs and out into the yard, kicking leaves and turning cartwheels until she was breathless. She checked her watch and realized with a new rush of excitement that Andy could be home by now and raced inside to call him. Then she hesitated. She was torn between sharing the news and being discreet. She'd save her news for the next day. It could wait.

A car door slammed in the driveway.

"Mom! Is that you? Is that really, really you?" Christine shouted as she ran to the door.

Mrs. Harter came in, laughing as Christine hopped around her. "Yes, it's really, really me. Whew," she said as she sat down. "I'm exhausted, and your bouncing around is making me even more tired. What's with the welcome wagon?"

"Oh, I don't know," Christine said. She noticed her mother's stained blue jeans and muddy hiking boots and asked, "Where've you been, Colorado?"

Her mother laughed shortly. "Hardly. No, I had a Conversation Council meeting, and we were looking over a preserve that's being threatened by noise pollution. Over by Hollow Oaks."

"Noise pollution? Who ever heard of that?" Christine asked. She sat down and tipped her chair back. "That's ridiculous."

"Christine, six legs on the floor, please," Mrs. Harter said, bending over to untie her shoelaces. She straightened up and kicked off her boots. "Have you got ants in your pants or something today?"

Christine thumped the chair back to the floor and closed her eyes. She wanted to tell her mother about the case. But accusing a teacher of a crime without evidence? Her mother would worry too much. Christine would tell her mother that she had good news and leave it at that.

She jumped up and got herself a glass of milk. Then she announced, "I know who the killer is."

Her mother raised her eyebrows. "Killer?"

Shrugging away the inconsistency, Christine continued, "Thief, killer, same thing. However," she added, holding up her hand, "I cannot at this time divulge the name of the murderer due to lack of concrete proof and admissible evidence. Suffice it to say that in due time, all will be revealed. And justice will be served."

Mrs. Harter stood up. "And if you'll help me peel some potatoes, dinner will also be served—in due time."

Christine stared at her mother's back,

openmouthed. "Aren't you going to make me tell you who it is?"

"Why?" her mother answered. "You just told me you couldn't 'divulge the name of the murderer,' so I am respecting your stated wish to remain silent."

"But, Mom, if you don't make me tell you, I'll be the next victim," Christine said.

Her mother turned around finally. "Excuse me?"

Taking another sip of her milk, Christine tucked her hair behind her ears. "Don't you see? In every mystery someone figures out who the murderer is, and then tells everyone he knows who the murderer is but won't tell. And then he gets killed, to keep him quiet. Happens every time." She nodded her head knowingly.

"Well, dear. If you choose to take such a course of action in the face of this rather fatal trend, then it's your decision." Mrs. Harter started sticking slivers of garlic into a roast. She smiled again. "But, seriously, Chris, if you do think you know who it is, be very sure. I know you'd regret accusing the wrong person."

"Oh, don't worry about that, Mom,"

Christine said. "I'm going to have all the evidence I need."

The next day during lunch, Christine dragged Andy out of the cafeteria to the front lawn, anxious to speak to him alone.

"What's up, Chris?" Andy asked. He was laughing as she pulled him along.

She stopped and turned to him triumphantly. "Answer me one question. Just one question, and I'll have solved the case."

She could see the look of wonder in his eyes, and she grinned. She was hardly able to stand still.

He nodded eagerly. "So go ahead. What's the one question?"

Christine flipped through the pages of her notepad until she came to her drawing of the stopwatch. She held it out to him.

Andy took the pad and stared at it silently for a moment. Finally he looked up, perplexed. "I don't get it. What's the question?"

Christine impatiently pointed to the picture. "What can you tell me about this? I mean, I don't want to lead you into the answer, I want—just tell me what your reaction to this drawing is."

He grinned. "I see. Well—I hate to say it, but

97

I don't think you're another Leonardo da Vinci, if that's what you mean."

"Andy! Come on!" Exasperated, she punched him in the arm as she took the drawing from him. She couldn't get angry; she was happier than she had ever been because she was sure Andy would confirm her suspicions. That confirmation would mean she could give in to her feelings for Andy.

"All right. That's the same kind of stopwatch we had. The kind that got stolen," he said.

Christine nodded. "What else?"

Andy looked back at the picture again. Slowly, a different look crossed his face. "Say, how did you draw this picture, anyway?" He looked at her. "I mean, you couldn't have seen it in a store."

Christine pressed her lips together, hardly daring to ask the next question. "Why?" she finally asked, trying to control her voice.

He shrugged. "Well, I was told that these Braun watches aren't sold in America at all. They're made in Germany, and only available in Europe. Ours was a gift from a guy who graduated from here about twenty years ago. Does a lot of business over there or something."

Christine carefully put the notepad into her

pocket. She kept her eyes on the ground. "And how many did he give the school?"

"Just one."

"ALL RIGHT!" Christine shouted. She threw her arms around Andy's neck.

Andy seemed surprised by her hug. He removed her arms gently from around his neck and held her away from himself, smiling at her. He laughed and asked, "What did I do right?"

Christine suddenly realized what a scene she had made and blushed. Her hands went automatically to her hair as she pulled away, and she stammered an apology. "I guess I'm acting like a maniac, huh?"

A funny look passed over Andy's face as he answered her. "No. I wouldn't say that at all."

The two stared at each other intently for a moment longer, until Andy finally broke the spell. "Now, do you want to tell me what this is all about? We are supposed to be partners, you know."

"Come on. Let's sit on the bench over here." Christine led the way, a little afraid to begin. "It's getting a lot colder, you know? I bet we'll be able to go skiing by Thanksgiving." She looked away, across the wide front lawn of the high school. She knew Andy was looking at her expectantly.

Christine turned to face him. "I know who the thief is."

"Great! Who is it?" Andy said anxiously.

Christine fiddled with the strap of her book bag, still stalling. She knew Andy wouldn't be exactly thrilled when she told him. She looked up into his blue eyes again. "It's Coach Keeler."

For a moment Andy stared at her, speechless. Then he said, "You're crazy. The coach's the last person in the world who would do it."

"Andy, please!" Christine grabbed his arm, drawing him back to her. "I know he did it. The watch was in his bag."

Andy shrugged off Christine's hand. He stood up and shook his head. "What would he want to steal it for. He's not poor or anything."

Christine shook her head. "I don't know! Maybe he's a klepto or something! You even suggested it the first time we met!"

"Oh, come on! You can't prove it, there's no way," Andy exclaimed. "I don't know where you get your bizarre ideas, but this one is just plain dumb. Keeler! The man's very straight and you think he's some kind of thief?"

"You just have to believe me, Andy. I know," Christine said.

He turned to her angrily. "Oh, yeah? Well, just how do you know? Did you see him?"

"No. But I—"

"Well, obviously you're just desperate to solve the case, so you picked anybody. You might as well have accused your brother— or—or me! You probably did it yourself. You're acting so dumb."

Christine stood up, angry and hurt. Hurt that Andy could let his loyalty to the coach make him cruel to her. "Dumb? I know he's got the stuff, and I think he's still got most of it right here. What better place to hide it than the place it was stolen from!" She drew a deep breath, trying to control her anger. She lowered her voice. "And I am going to find it. I'm going to search his office on Friday night after dinner and get all the proof I need. And if you don't like it—" She paused, her anger drained from her.

Andy's jaw was clenched tightly. Christine could see the muscles and tendons of his neck straining, and she wondered suddenly if he was trying not to cry, too.

She reached out to touch his arm; he flinched as if he'd been burned. "I don't believe you," he said, every word slow and distinct.

Christine leaned down to pick up her book bag, and straightened up slowly. "Fine. I learned pretty recently that the truth isn't always what you hope it'll be. But if you can't even accept the idea that Keeler *might* have done it, then I guess we don't have much else to say to each other."

Andy's back was still turned toward her. She gulped hard and tried not to cry. "Goodbye, Andy."

She stayed a moment longer, hoping that he'd, at least, say goodbye. But he didn't. On trembling legs, Christine turned and walked toward school.

"Hey, Chris! Wait up!" a girl's voice called.

Teri came running toward her, ponytail bouncing. Christine stopped and stared hard at the ground. She didn't want Teri to see how upset she was.

"Hey. Wasn't that Andy Mellon you were talking to?" Teri asked as she fell into step beside Christine. "Something going on between you two? I've seen you together a lot."

Christine managed a weak, ironic laugh. "Hardly," she said.

Her friend looked at her and shrugged. "If you say so. Oh, Chris. Guess what? I can't believe it."

Sighing, Christine asked, "What is it?"

"Yesterday after practice your brother, the one and only Danny Harter, talked to me for about five minutes outside the gym." She shifted her books and pulled a strand of fly-away hair from her face. "Anything in it, do you think? I mean, do you think that's a good sign?"

"I don't know," she muttered.

"Oh, come on, Christine. You've got to know. He's your brother. How significant is it?"

Christine looked away, sure that Teri would be able to see the tears in her eyes. "I guess that's fairly promising. He has a tendency not to talk to anyone who isn't on the team, you know."

Teri laughed. She was apparently unaware of Christine's unhappiness. "I know! And he talked about football to me! But I don't care. Anyway, I had to tell you. I'm late. Bye!"

Christine watched Teri walk away. Then she broke down and let the tears stream down her cheeks, hoping she could stop before lunch was over.

Only that morning, Christine had been so happy with Andy. Now she felt miserable—and utterly alone.

Chapter Nine

As Friday approached, the enormity of what Christine had planned to do hit her. She had to break into the gym and search Coach Keeler's office. She wasn't sure how to do it. She was ready to go on Friday evening, but, as she sat on her bed with her Polaroid camera, she still had no plan.

Danny paused in her doorway on his way downstairs. "You OK, Chris?"

She looked up at him and then back at the camera in her lap. Then she stood up, pulled him into her room, and shut the door.

"Danny, I need to talk to you. This is really important," Christine said.

Danny looked curious. "I'm going to do something stupid tonight, and I want you to know in case I need to be bailed out," she announced grimly.

A slow smile spread over Danny's face. "Really? Go on."

Christine took a deep breath and started in. "I have to break into the gym and search it tonight."

For a moment her brother simply stared at her, then he laughed. "That is totally awesome, Chris. I didn't know you had it in you."

"Well, just don't tell Mom and Dad, whatever you do."

"Hey—why are you searching the gym anyway?" he asked. "Finally got yourself a suspect?"

Christine knew her brother liked Keeler; but she was sure he didn't have any special feelings for him as Andy did. "Well, I'm pretty sure Coach Keeler is the guy who's stealing stuff," she answered.

Danny looked at her in amazement. "Awesome. Totally awesome," he said at last.

"Danny, can't you say anything but 'awesome'?" Christine asked. She nervously checked her camera for the seventh time, to make sure it had film in it. "It makes you sound completely dumb."

He shrugged and stood up. "How about 'outrageous'? Hey, I can't help it—it is awesome. When are you going?"

Christine stood up too. "Now. If I'm not home by—I don't know. I mean, I don't know how long it'll take."

Her brother opened the door. "Why don't I just pick you up at the gym at eleven?"

Christine was relieved that he had made the decision for her. She smiled and nodded. "OK. Eleven. Wish me luck?"

He smiled back, but was suddenly serious. "Hey, Chris, how are you getting in, anyway?"

She was embarrassed. "I—actually, I don't know," she admitted sheepishly. "I sort of thought I'd take care of that when I got there."

Danny dug into one pocket of his jeans. "Here," he said as he took one key from the ring he carried. "I'm not really supposed to have this, but it kind of gets handed down from one captain to the next. It's sort of unofficial."

Christine took the key and smiled gratefully at Danny as she put it in her pocket. Her brother continued. "It's for the outside door— and if you tell anybody I'll kill you," he finished gruffly. "So don't get caught."

She grinned. "Don't worry, I won't."

Fortunately, Mr. and Mrs. Harter were out

at a dinner party, so Christine didn't have to answer any tricky questions about her plans for the evening.

Danny dropped her off at school on his way to the movies. "Sure you don't want me to come with you?" he asked. "I've seen this movie already, so it's no sweat."

"No thanks," Christine answered, opening the door and getting out. She poked her head back in. "We professional detectives don't like to work with amateurs, you know. They get in the way."

She heard Danny laugh as she slammed the door. But as he pulled away from the curb, Christine started to lose her nerve. She felt very much alone.

She squared her shoulders and glanced around her. The campus looked so utterly alien: it was dark and so quiet that it was almost impossible to imagine it bright and noisy with hundreds of high school kids. She walked quickly to the gym, looking nervously over her shoulder from time to time.

"Cool out, Harter. There are no bogeymen here," she chided herself.

As she stepped up to the outer door of the gym building, a tall figure emerged from the shadows. Christine's heart jumped; she stifled a scream and backed up. "Who's there?"

"Chris? Chris, it's me," Andy said as he stepped forward into the dim light. "Sorry. Did I scare you?"

Christine was reluctant to admit just how badly he had startled her. "No." Her voice faltered but then grew stronger. "No, not really. What are you doing here anyway?"

"Well—" He sounded a little embarrassed, Christine thought. Andy continued, "I couldn't let you do it alone. I've been waiting here since it got dark. Besides, I've been thinking about, well, about you. What you said the other day . . ." he stopped in midsentence.

In the darkness neither could make out the other's face at all. The sudden, surprising prick of tears in her eyes made Christine glad of the shadows. She didn't know whether the tears had been prompted by relief or his caring. But his few words made her think that the romantic dream she'd been mourning might not be dead after all.

Andy's voice was husky as he said, "We're partners, Christine. I do want to know the truth—about everything," he added.

Everything? Did he mean the truth about

how much she liked him? She convinced herself that he was only talking about the case. She forced her voice to be steady and businesslike as she replied, "I'm glad you came. Let's get going. I've got a key to the outside door."

Keenly aware of Andy's presence close behind her, Christine fumbled with the doorknob; her hand was surprisingly shaky. *It's the case* she told herself. *I'm about to crack it.* But deep down she knew that the case wasn't making her hand shake.

"Here, let me help you," came Andy's voice, close to her ear. His hand brushed hers as he took the key from her. The lock clicked, and Christine slipped gratefully inside. Andy came in behind her and pulled the door shut.

"Is it safe to turn on a light, do you think?" Christine whispered.

"Let's wait till we get into the locker room," Andy replied in the darkness. "There's only one window in there, and its in the cage. High up. I don't think anyone will notice the light. Here, give me your hand."

It took Christine a few false tries to find Andy's hand. It was thrilling to be in the dark with Andy. They made their way toward the locker room door. Then Andy opened the door and they were inside.

Andy hit a switch. They were bathed in light and stood blinking and trying to adjust their eyes to the glare. For the first time since they had met outside, they could see each other. Christine was struck again by Andy's good looks. She was suddenly embarrassed, and she could tell that Andy was flustered, too.

"Andy, I—"

"I'm sor—"

Both of them stopped; Andy started again. "I'm sorry I acted like such a jerk, Christine."

"No," she protested. "I should have told you in a better way, that's all."

He shook his head. "You shouldn't have had to do that. I just didn't want to believe you—I wouldn't even accept it as a possibility. I was angry with you for making me see what a dope I was being." He held out his hand. "Partners again?"

She took his hand and smiled back. "Partners." Afraid of the electricity between them, Christine let go of his hand and turned away. "Maybe we can change the motto to 'Harter and Mellon, we get our felon.' How's that?" she asked over her shoulder, determined to keep the conversation light.

Andy laughingly followed her down the rows of lockers and benches, until they finally arrived at the cage. "Let's check this out first," Christine said, grasping the chicken wire and peering through.

"Why?" Andy glanced over at Keeler's office. "Wouldn't the goods be in there?"

Christine threw him a mischievous grin. "Probably, but I want to show you something." She swung the door open and strode inside. She went to the tall carton of basketballs and squeezed behind it. "Thifi whif uh waff." Her voice drifted out, muffled.

"What?" Andy asked.

She leaned out again. "This is where I was— when you caught me in here."

Andy smiled appreciatively. "So that's where you were hiding. I knew there was someone in here—that was why I came back— but I couldn't figure out where."

"You just 'sensed another presence,' as they say?" Christine asked teasingly.

He grinned. "Let's say I felt something in the air." His eyes became serious. "Maybe I knew something important was about to happen."

"Like catching the criminal?" Christine said, deliberately ignoring his tone.

"Like meeting you."

Christine scrambled out, keeping a few boxes between herself and Andy; her camera hit her hip as she maneuvered through the clutter. "Hey," she said, holding it up. "Smile!" She pressed the shutter release, and the photograph was automatically ejected from the camera.

"Hey, no fair!" Andy objected. "Here, let me see that!" He reached over and took the photograph from her hand. "No picture yet. These things freak me out, the way the colors appear while you watch."

Christine sat down where she could see the small square. They stared at the photograph as Andy's face became clearer and clearer. They laughed.

"Boy, talk about unphotogenic," Christine said giggling. "You look like the monster from the black lagoon. Guess I shouldn't have caught you off guard."

He arched his eyebrows sarcastically. "Oh, yeah? Well, let me try." He took the camera from her, and sat down next to her. He held the Polaroid at arms' length, facing them. He casually draped his free arm around her shoulders. "Now watch the birdie—if I can do this with one hand—ah!" A click and a flash left them blinking, and Christine held on to the photograph as soon as it developed.

She peeked at Andy from under her lashes as they sat together. He was staring at the picture, his arm still around her. Their two faces slowly emerged from the colorless background; Andy's looked much more handsome this time, and Christine had a somewhat surprised look on her face, as though she had never expected to be in such a picture with Andy Mellon.

"There. I think that's a good one," Andy said, holding the picture out. "Looks like we were made for each other," he added, looking at her tenderly.

"Isn't it about time we went to look in the office?" Christine stood up and hurried away from Andy. She was afraid to give in to the temptation of Andy's tone.

Andy sighed and followed her.

"I hope this door is unlocked, because I don't think this key works in it," Christine said nervously as she approached the heavy door.

"I don't have one, either," Andy answered from behind her. But the door was unlocked. Christine opened it, looking at Andy with relief.

He waved his hand toward the office. "After you, miss."

Christine bowed her head. "Thank you, sir." She went into the office and flipped the light switch as she passed through the door.

They stood there, suddenly feeling like real intruders.

"That's his desk," Andy said.

"I can see that," Christine said. She walked over to it and looked at the cluttered surface.

"Now what?" Andy asked.

Christine turned back to the desk. "We search it, I guess." She smiled nervously. "I have to admit, this is my first search. Just don't tell anyone."

The tension was broken, and they both laughed. "Let's start with the drawers," Andy said, joining her at that end of the room. "But I still can't believe he'd leave anything here—"

Christine nodded. "I know, but if he kept that watch with him, he might still have the other stuff around." She pulled open a drawer and sifted through the loose contents with her index finger. "Paper clips, receipts, shoelaces, Band-Aids. Exciting stuff," she concluded sarcastically.

Andy opened the bottom drawer. "Exciting stuff? Look," he said.

Christine looked, let out a gasp. "Those rings! Those are the class rings!"

"Yes, they are," Andy said. He leaned on the desk and let out a deep breath. He looked down at the floor.

Christine's heart went out to him; he was taking the truth hard. "Sorry, Andy," she said gently.

"Well, I guess there's no question about it now," he said.

Christine remained silent.

"Well, let's take the pictures," Andy said, squaring his shoulders. "And then we can get out of here." He took his jacket off and threw it on a chair. His keys jingled in the pockets as the jacket landed.

"We might find some of the other stuff, too. He must have just assumed that no one would suspect him," Christine said, as she focused her camera. "With these pictures and my testimony that I saw him with the stopwatch—"

"I didn't believe you when you told me he had it," Andy said.

She turned. "That's OK."

"No, it's not. I'm sorry I didn't trust you," he said. He shook his head. "OK. Let's get some shots."

Christine snapped a picture of the rings;

further search turned up the watches and other things that had disappeared. All of the photos went into Christine's pocket.

Their final task was to put everything back as it had been. Christine set the camera on top of Andy's jacket.

"Let's take another look around the cage," Andy suggested. "I might be able to tell if anything else is gone. And we've got to get our pictures out of there."

They left the office and re-entered the cage. Christine felt nervous and stayed close to Andy. He grabbed her arm once. Was he a little nervous too? They wandered among the rows of boxes and piles of uniforms.

"It's actually kind of creepy in here, you know?" Christine said, looking into a shadowy corner.

"Fear not, fair maiden. I shall protect you," Andy said laughing.

"I'll probably end up protecting *you*," Christine shot back.

Passing the spot where they had taken the first pictures, Christine found the photographs there and picked them up, smiling at their images. "Neither one of us is going to win any awards for—"

A creak and the sound of the cage door

closing interrupted her. They looked at each other, paralyzed.

"That was the cage door!" Andy shouted.

They raced back to the entrance of the cage. But the lock had already been secured. They heard the door to the coaches office being pulled closed and the opening and closing of the desk drawers. As they stood looking out of the chicken wire, Coach Keeler backed out of his office, a shopping bag in his hand. He didn't look at the cage, but instead moved to the door of the locker room and made his escape.

Christine looked at Andy in panic. And then the lights went out.

Chapter Ten

"It's no use." Andy jumped down from the stack of boxes they had piled against the wall. "The window only opens about three inches because there are steel bars beyond it. If I could take the hinges off the frame for the bars we might be able to open the window enough to get out. But there aren't any tools in here." He wiped his hands on his jeans.

Dim light from a distant street lamp filtered in through the small window. Christine and Andy stared glumly at each other.

They had tried to open the cage door, but Andy's keys to the cage were in his jacket, which he had forgotten in the office. For once, the door of the gym's storeroom was securely locked.

"What are we going to do now?" Christine wondered out loud as they sat down under the window.

"We'll have to try to catch someone's attention," Andy said, glancing at the window.

Christine laughed grimly. "One of the many hundreds of people wandering around campus at night?" she asked.

"Go easy on the sarcasm, will you? I'm just trying to help," Andy said.

Christine touched Andy's arm. "I'm sorry, Andy. I'm so insensitive sometimes. I didn't mean it," she said contritely.

She could see his smile in the dim light. "No problem," Andy said amicably. He stretched his long legs out and sighed. "So, I guess Keeler isn't exactly the great guy I thought he was, huh? Shows you what a great judge of character I am."

Christine shook her head. "There was no reason for you to think anything else, Andy. He really seems like a nice guy. I would have thought so, too, when I talked to him, except that I already suspected he might be the thief."

"Well, he's got us where he wants us. You can bet he took the evidence with him," Andy said grimly.

She couldn't help being mad herself, though, when she thought of Keeler locking them in. "How do you think he knew we were here, anyway?" she mused out loud.

"I don't know. Maybe it was just a coincidence. Maybe he came back to get some of the stuff and saw us taking pictures."

Christine perked up suddenly. "But we still have the pictures! I put them in my pocket! We can definitely nail him. To think I almost left them in his office," she said.

Christine pulled the photographs out of her back pocket, and then stood up to stand nearer to the light. "I hope these count as evidence," she muttered, flipping through the pictures. "I guess it's pretty clear that it's Keeler's office, but I mean, he could say we put the stuff there to frame him.

"It'd be just like him to say that," she continued. "Especially since—" She broke off.

"Since what?" Andy asked.

Christine sighed. "Since I think he was trying to make it look like you were doing it." She stared at Andy.

"How do you know?" he asked quietly.

"It just added up," Christine said. "It's just a theory."

"He could also deny locking us in here," he

said. "But when you think about it, it would be pretty crazy for the two of us to steal the stuff, put it in Keeler's office, lock ourselves in here, and then accuse him." He shook his head. "That would be pretty weird."

Christine nodded her head and sat down. "You're pretty good at this. It's a good thing we're partners because this town ain't big enough for two gumshoes, see."

"Who are you calling a gumshoe, lady?" Andy asked, imitating her Humphery Bogart voice and sitting beside her.

She could see Andy looking at her in the darkness, smiling. "What's so funny?" she asked.

His smile broadened. "I was just thinking— here I am, locked in the cage with Christine Harter. Locked in by a man I trusted. Can't get out, no one knows we're here, and I don't really mind all that much."

Christine felt herself blushing.

"And besides," he continued, "now you can't keep avoiding me."

"What do you mean?" Christine stammered, although she knew exactly what he meant.

"This," he said. His hand caressed her face. Then he pulled her closer and kissed her.

Christine closed her eyes and felt the soft pressure of his lips on hers. She thought her pounding heart would burst.

He pulled away, and she rested her forehead against his shoulder. "Oh, Andy," she whispered. "I thought you hated me after what happened."

"Hated you?" Andy laughed, completely taken aback. "I've been crazy about you ever since I caught you in the locker room." He shook his head in amazement. "You're one in a million, Christine. And I love you. I mean it."

She leaned back against the wall and drew her knees up to her chin. She sighed, looking at him, and they were silent for a few moments.

Finally, Christine shook her head. "I guess you must have been pretty surprised to find a girl in here, huh?"

"Surprised?" Andy laughed again and kissed the tip of her nose. "Actually," he continued, "my first reaction was to think that you were the thief. Even though I liked you right away, I wasn't sure you were innocent."

"What made you change your mind?" Christine asked.

He touched her hand. "The more I got to

know you the more I knew you couldn't be a criminal."

Christine felt herself blushing again and felt deeply ashamed for ever having doubted Andy. "I—I have someting to tell you."

"What?" he prompted her gently.

"This is so embarrassing," she said.

He laughed softly. "Come on. Just tell me."

"Well, I thought *you* were the thief!" she finished in a rush.

"What?" Andy said, sounding shocked. "What made you think that?"

"Actually, I think it had something to do with the book I was reading before I started the case," she admitted. "This guy murdered his father, and I knew he did it because he was so handsome and no one suspected he had a motive."

"So?"

Christine hid her face in her hands, half-joking, half-serious. Andy pulled her hands away and held them. Christine said, "Boy, this is so dumb. I can't believe I'm telling you this."

"Just tell me, will you?" Andy urged her.

She sighed. "So I had this formula that whoever was doing this job was handsome and somebody nobody would ever suspect."

Andy laughed, obviously surprised. "Who, me?" She searched his face for any sign of indignation or anger. She said, "Isn't that dumb?"

"No." He grinned. "Well, it is a little. But there are plenty of other guys—the whole team. Why me?"

"I found out you were responsible for the equipment, and you told me you were broke, and then you were gone at all the crucial moments and—"

"Chris," he said, interrupting her.

She looked into his shadowed face.

"I love you. I really do. But you're crazy. You read too many books."

"I do not!" she exclaimed indignantly. "That was all good, solid detective work!"

"But it was wrong!"

Christine couldn't help laughing. "Oh, I'll get you!" She put her hands gently around his neck and kissed him.

"Boy, that'll teach me," he said when they broke apart. Andy wrapped his arms around her and leaned against the wall, cradling her. With a blissful sigh, Christine relaxed against him and closed her eyes.

Andy moved slightly. "If we only had a

screwdriver—even my keys—maybe I could undo the hinges on the bars on the window.

"Keys?" Christine slapped her hand to her forehead. "I'm so dense. I have the key to the outside door. We can use that to loosen the hinge, right?"

He turned, his hand outstretched. "Here, let me try it."

Digging in her pocket, Christine pulled out her brother's key and handed it to Andy. He climbed up the boxes and began working.

"Oh, you know what else I forgot?" Christine said. "My brother is going to be here at eleven o'clock." She paused for a moment, watching Andy wrestle with the keys. "But I don't have my watch on. Do you?"

"No," Andy said.

Andy's face was now lit by the window. Christine leaned one shoulder against the wall and looked up at him. She loved him. She was sure of that. And watching him, she felt amazed that he felt the same way. His kisses had been so sweet.

She was jolted back to reality by a new thought.

"Andy! We don't just have to get out of here for ourselves. Keeler could be running away, and no one knows but us!" Clambering breathlessly up the boxes next to Andy, she continued, "Can't you hurry?"

"I'm—hurry-ing," he grunted through clenched teeth. He was trying—without much success—to loosen the hinge with the edge of the key.

"Just one—darn!" Andy said. He held out the key. It was gouged along one side, and bent at the top. Christine took it silently. Andy jumped down and held out his hand to help her to the floor. They stood there staring at each other, momentarily defeated.

With a rueful smile, Christine broke the gloomy silence. "Well, now I don't want to get out, because my brother will kill me when he sees this key."

"Chris, I'm sorry." Andy took her in his arms.

Against his chest Christine muttered "It's not your fault. It's Keeler's." She lifted her face so she could see his. "We can get out, you know. We just have to use our heads. I'm going to go have another look at the door," she said.

When Andy found her, a few minutes later, she was standing with her fingers grasping the chicken wire. She was staring out like a prisoner in a cell.

"Getting claustrophobic?" he asked.

She remained staring straight ahead for a moment without speaking. Then she said, "Do you see that fire alarm?" looking at the opposite wall. Andy nodded.

"Can we trigger it?" she asked. Christine stared hard at the alarm. "Is that the kind—no, you don't have to pull a lever. See? You just break the glass, and there's a button to push. Maybe we could throw something at it?" She looked hopefully at Andy.

He held up his hands. "Whoa! I'm no pitcher, you know. And, anyway how can we get a ball through these holes. They're too small.

"Andy, come on. We've got to try. Hey, look. If we could pull one staple loose on the frame of the door, we could squeeze our hands through."

They finally pulled a staple free after fifteen minutes and bent the wire back.

"I know I saw a box of baseballs while I was scrounging around. Hold on a sec," Andy said.

Christine watched as Andy disappeared back into the shadows. But he quickly returned, holding a large carton out in front of him.

"Step right up, ladies and gents! Or should I

say just lady?" Andy opened the box and tossed a baseball to Christine. "Care to try your luck? Hit the target and get a free ride on the fire engine!"

Giggling hysterically, Christine squeezed the baseball and her hand through the small opening as Andy kept up the carnival-barker routine. Christine was able to get enough elbow room to swing and let the baseball fly toward the alarm.

·It missed.

Her second and third balls hit the box, but the glass didn't break. "We need something heavier to break the glass," she said.

"OK," Andy agreed, turning away. "I'll see what I can find."

He was gone for a moment, but returned shortly with a horseshoe.

"Can you believe this?" he asked, laughing. " 'What did you do in gym today, son?' 'Oh, we played horseshoes. It was really swell.' This has probably been around for twenty years."

Taking the horseshoe, Christine turned back to the door. "Is this the only one?" she asked, turning back.

Andy shrugged. "It's the only one I found."

With a deep breath, Christine turned and

put her arm through the hole. "Here goes, then, One shot."

She drew her arm back and tossed the horseshoe underhand to the alarm box. The heavy piece of iron splintered the glass and pushed in the alarm button.

A shrill bell went off. "You did it!" yelled Andy above the noise. "You got the bull's-eye!" He swung her around in a hug. Then they covered their ears. The noise was deafening.

A siren became audible through the din, and the two ran back to the window and scrambled onto the boxes. Christine waved her sweater out the window, and they both screamed for all they were worth.

"In here!" Andy yelled.

"We're in here! Help!" Christine shouted.

Finally the brilliant beam of a flashlight slashed through the darkness, and an adult voice boomed out, "WHAT'S GOING ON IN HERE!"

Chapter Eleven

"Thank you very much, officer. Good night." Christine heard her father's voice in the hall. Then she heard the front door close.

She looked up from her mug of hot chocolate to find her mother watching her curiously.

"Well," said Mr. Harter as he came back into the den, rubbing his hands together. "You've had quite a night, young lady."

It was long past midnight, and Christine, Danny, and their parents—who were still dressed up from their dinner party—had spent over an hour with the police. They'd answered dozens of questions and explained everything over and over. Christine was exhausted but she felt curiously alert, too. She looked from her mother to her father and back nervously, fully expecting to get a lecture.

When her mother finally spoke, Christine was surprised at the softness of her tone. "I think we've all had quite a night," she said. "Why don't we all just go to bed."

Christine looked across the room at Danny but he just shrugged.

"Good night, kids," Christine's mother said. She and Mr. Harter started toward the stairs. Suddenly, Mrs. Harter turned back, bent down, and hugged Christine fiercely. "Oooh. I don't know whether to ground you or buy you an extravagant present." She turned away quickly and walked out of the room.

Christine's father smiled at her. "You gave your mother quite a scare." He sighed and shook his head. "Me, too, pumpkin. Good night. Danny, turn the lights off before you go upstairs."

After he left, Christine and Danny just sat in the quiet room. Neither of them said anything for a moment. Slowly, a grin stole over Danny's face, and pretty soon he was laughing. He laughed louder and louder, until Christine began giggling herself. They both laughed until their sides ached and tears streamed down their faces. Finally, clutching their stomachs, they calmed down.

Danny wiped his eyes. "Chris, you are something else."

Christine took a deep breath and grinned. "Thanks, big brother." She leaned her head over the back of her chair. "I can't figure someting out, though, Dan, I mean, there was an awful lot of confusion when the cops got to the gym. But what I can't figure out—did you call them? Is that why they arrived so quickly after the alarm went off?"

Danny nodded. "When you weren't outside the gym at eleven like we agreed and I didn't see any lights inside or anything, I got worried. I figured you were in trouble, and I figured you wouldn't mind if I told everyone where you were," he said.

"Boy, I bet Mom and Dad freaked out when you told them what I was doing!" Christine said. Picturing her parents' faces, she wanted to laugh, but she also felt guilty.

Danny laughed. "Are you kidding? Mom turned all white and said 'my baby!' And Dad said, 'Don't worry, Bev. We'll handle it.' "

Christine smiled and picked up her mug of cocoa again. "Well, I'm glad you did call the police. But," she added, "the cops would have turned up pretty soon anyway. With that alarm going off, how could they have missed us? I thought we'd go deaf in there."

"Speaking of 'we', since when have you and Andy Mellon been hanging out together?" Danny asked.

"I don't know. Not very long," Christine said, trying to sound nonchalant but blushing, nevertheless.

"Yeah, well, you looked like you knew each other pretty well. But far be it for *me* to poke into someone else's business." Danny stood up. I'm beat—little sisters always running to their big brothers when they're in trouble. It's a tiring responsibility."

Christine threw a pillow at him, but he ducked. The pillow landed outside in the hall.

"But really," he said, leaning through the door and picking up the pillow. "Thanks for catching him. Keeler, I mean. You don't know what it was like, not knowing. Well, it's over now. Thanks." He smiled and threw the pillow back to her. "Good night, Chris." She heard him thump up the steps.

Christine was alone in the den with her lukewarm cocoa and her jumbled thoughts. She gulped the rest of the chocolate and set the mug down on a table. Curling up in the big, overstuffed chair, she went over the events of the evening.

When the police and the fire department arrived—with her parents and Danny right behind them—they managed to break the lock to the cage. As soon as they were free, Christine and Andy were bombarded with questions and accusations. Sometime during the confusion, she'd lost track of Andy. She looked for him, but her parents had hustled her into the car before she found him.

Suddenly Christine felt lonely. She missed Andy very badly. She missed his calmness and the cute way he smiled. And now that she knew he cared for her, she missed that, too. Christine tried to remember exactly what he'd said to her, what they'd talked about. But she ended up falling asleep in the chair instead.

She was awakened hours later by the distant ringing of the telephone, and simultaneously became aware of coffee brewing and bacon frying. She uncurled herself painfully from the chair.

Her mother was just hanging up the phone as Christine walked into the kitchen, rubbing her eyes. "Who was that?" she asked as she poured herself some orange juice. "It's still pretty early, isn't it?"

"No, it's not that early. It's eight o'clock." Mrs. Harter said, smiling as she sat down. "That was Lieutenant Armstrong—you remember him from last night."

Christine nodded and waited silently for her mother to continue.

"Well, it seems that the police decided to get Coach Keeler's side of the story—after all, your accusation sounded pretty wild in spite of the evidence." Mrs. Harter shook her head as she remembered just how crazy the previous night had been. "Anyway," she went on, "as soon as they got to his house, Keeler broke down and confessed. It seems the poor man has some pretty serious psychological problems. Apparently, he just steals for the thrill and challenge of it—the value of whatever he steals isn't important at all. He doesn't really care what he takes."

Christine bit her lip, thinking over this latest piece of information. "I guess that's why he left all the stuff hanging around. It doesn't make much sense, though."

"No, sweetheart, it doesn't. Richard Keeler is going to need a lot of counseling to figure out why he feels the need to steal."

"Hmm. You know it's funny," Christine mused, taking a sip of juice. "I never knew his first name before. Huh." She stared into her glass.

Mrs. Harter reached across the table and took her daughter's hand. "You're so terrific. I'm very proud of you for not gloating about solving the case. You certainly have earned the privilege."

Christine looked into her mother's eyes; for the first time in days, she didn't feel she had to hide anything. She looked down at the table again and blushed as she asked, "Did you see that guy that was with me last night?"

Repressing a smile, her mother nodded. "Tall, *very* handsome, very intelligent looking?"

Christine sighed and smiled. "That's the one. That's Andy Mellon, and he's—" She looked around as she tried to find the right words to describe Andy and the way she felt about him.

Mrs. Harter picked up her coffee cup. "I'd call him awesome, wouldn't you?"

They both laughed and exchanged a look which clearly showed how well they understood each other. They were still giggling when Mr. Harter came in, followed closely by Danny.

"What's so funny?" Danny asked. "It's too

early to be laughing." He walked over to a cupboard to get some cereal.

"It's not so early!" Mrs. Harter replied as her husband kissed her. "Good morning, Frank."

" 'Morning, Bev." Mr. Harter sat down and reached for a section of the newspaper. He opened it up, disappearing behind the pages. Mrs. Harter used a fork to push the paper aside so she could see her husband. "They got him, Frank."

"That's nice, Bevvy," he said.

Christine shrugged. "All in a day's work, I guess."

"Got who?" Danny asked as he spooned Cheerios into his mouth. "Who's him?"

"Coach Keeler, your fearless leader," Christine answered, trying to sound casual. In truth, she felt a strange mixture of elation and sadness. She and Andy had found each other and a compulsive thief had been stopped because of her detective work. But she had also proven that a man Danny had trusted was a criminal. She decided she needed to be alone.

"Excuse me," she said as she stood up. "I'm going back to sleep—in my bed this time."

As she left the room, she heard the newspaper rustle and her father ask, "Who did you say you got, honey?" Christine smiled as she made her way upstairs.

But the real reason she wanted to be alone had nothing to do with sleep. It was because she was sure Andy would call, and she needed time to think about what she would say to him.

"Oh, Andy," she said. "I love you so much." She sat on her bed, and stared out the window. She was still tired, but it was a warm, sleepy tiredness. It was nothing like the exhaustion she'd felt the night before.

Feeling content and at peace for the first time since she had started the case, she snuggled down into the covers with a new mystery. "Now, let's see who did it this time," she said as she opened the paperback with relish. Phiz joined her with a soft thump on her bed, and her feeling of happiness was complete.

At noon she put the book down, and glanced at her clock. She decided that Andy must be sleeping late, and sternly forbade herself to feel impatient. Christine picked up the book again.

By four o'clock she had finished the book—at least as far as she was concerned, since she had solved the mystery—and Andy still hadn't called. "Come on, you dope. Pick up the phone," she muttered, fixing herself a sandwich in the kitchen. She had just taken a huge bite of peanut butter and jelly, when the phone rang.

"Huwo?" she said as she tried to chew and swallow at the same time.

"Hello, may I speak to your mother please?" a feminine voice said. Christine called her mother to the phone and waited impatiently while Mrs. Harter talked. The phone call dragged on for five, and then ten minutes, and Christine was sure that Andy was trying to call her right then. She shifted impatiently from foot to foot, making agonized faces at her mother.

"If you don't stop that right now I'll disown you," Mrs. Harter whispered with one hand over the mouthpiece.

Christine stomped angrily upstairs and spent two hours trying on all her clothes. She decided that she hated everything she owned. Later, at dinner, everyone talked about Coach Keeler and Christine's detective work. They asked her all sorts of questions about how she'd figured everything out. She answered them halfheartedly.

"I realized one thing, though," she said as she poured herself some more milk.

"What's that, honey?" her father asked.

"Well, being a detective isn't exactly what I thought it would be."

Mr. and Mrs. Harter looked across the table at each other. "In what way?" her mother asked.

Christine thought about it for a moment. "Well, I always thought you had to remove yourself from the case—you know, emotionally. So you can be objective."

Her mother nodded.

"And you do, but you can't. Does that make sense?" She looked at her parents, hoping they'd understand.

Mr. Harter nodded. "It's one of the great ironies of life, my dear." He looked at his wife and smiled. "You usually have to walk a very fine line between caring too much and not caring enough when you deal with other people. Finding it—and staying on it—is the most important skill you'll ever learn. Some people never do," he added. He tousled his daughter's blond hair affectionately.

The rest of the evening was uneventful. To Christine. the most significant event was what didn't happen—Anyd still hadn't called. And she was starting to get worried.

"What are you doing tonight?" she asked

Danny when she noticed him brushing his teeth after dinner.

He scowled at his reflection and bared his teeth. "Got a date," he told her.

"Oh. Who's the lucky girl?"

"Uh—Teri Hutchinson," Danny said casually.

Christine was stunned. "You're kidding, right." She leaned against the bathroom door-jamb, and shook her head. "I don't believe it." She squeezed close to one side as her brother brushed past her.

"Well, believe it, Miss Brilliant Detective."

Danny was down the stairs and gone before Christine moved. "How does she do it?" she wondered out loud. "Teri just has to look at a guy and he asks her out." She finally went to bed, depressed and confused, at ten o'clock.

Andy didn't call on Sunday, either. Several times Christine stood by the telephone, unable to decide whether or not she should call him.

"There's no reason why a girl shouldn't call a guy," she told herself.

"But if he doesn't want to call me, what good will my calling him do?" she argued back.

She seesawed back and forth on the question all day before she realized there could be a terrible reason why he hadn't called. What if Friday night had been just a flirtation for Andy? What if it had been just a game, because they were locked in together? Christine felt sick at the thought.

"He said he loved me. He couldn't have been lying. He just couldn't."

But when she went to bed Sunday night without hearing from him, she couldn't think of any other reason. She was sure that he wasn't thinking about her. Not at all.

Chapter Twelve

Christine left for school on Monday morning feeling depressed and nervous. She didn't know what people would be saying, but she knew that she'd have a lot of questions to answer.

Her fears were well-founded. Seconds after she got to school, Christine was surrounded at her locker by classmates.

"Christine! Did Coach Keeler really pull a gun on you?" one girl asked.

"Uh, no—" Christine started.

A tall boy laughed and interrupted her. "A gun? I thought he tied them up and started a fire in the gym."

"No way! Keeler and Andy Mellon got into a

fight, but the coach escaped," another student said.

"I heard you were on the news the other night. What was it like?"

"Christine! Can I interview you for the school paper?"

"Didn't you freak out? Keeler's some kind of a psycho-killer, right?"

Chris looked frantically from face to face. The kids around her were pushing and shoving one another. Everyone wanted to tell his or her version of the story; no one was paying any attention to Christine. Feeling as if she might be trampled, Christine wished she could get inside her locker. She looked around in desperation.

"Come on," a voice said in her ear. Teri pulled her friend out of the mob to safety. The two girls ran out of the building and sat down on the grass under a tree.

"Whew!" Teri gasped as she dropped her books at her side. "What a mob scene! It's worse than a Bruce Springsteen concert."

"I know. Tell me this is going to stop." Christine lay back on the grass, one arm over her face. She mumbled through her sleeve. "I wish they'd leave me alone. I hate this."

Teri moved Christine's arm away from her

face. "Oh, come on, Chris. That's the price of fame. You always wanted to be a famous detective, and now you are. I guess you'll just have to get used to it."

"Thanks a lot, Ter!" Chris sat up, smiling. "Why can't I just be a detective and let you be my public relations manager or something? You'd be great."

Teri gave her friend a playful look. "How about letting Andy be your public relations man? He's got the inside story, not me."

The nagging ache that had been haunting Christine all weekend suddenly returned, and she looked away.

"Chris?" Teri's voice was gentle.

She just couldn't turn around and look at her friend. Teri was too cheerful and Christine wanted to be depressed. She wanted to think about the boy she liked so much, who didn't seem to care about her at all. And she couldn't hide her feelings from Teri.

Teri gently turned her around and looked anxiously into her eyes. "What's wrong, Chris? Can't you tell me?"

Pressing her lips together, Christine looked searchingly into her friend's face. She wished she knew Teri's secret formula for attracting boys. But all she saw was sympathy and concern.

Christine tried to laugh. "Nothing's wrong. Really. I just haven't really recovered from all the excitement yet. Honest."

The first period bell rang, and both girls quickly picked up their books and hurried to class.

"See you later, OK?"

Christine nodded and went in to her class. She tried to tell herself that Andy would probably catch up with her later, but she didn't believe he really would.

Students and teachers continued to ask Christine questions all day. It was obvious to her that they also assumed she and Andy were an item. But no one seemed to notice that Christine and Andy weren't together. She couldn't figure out why she hadn't run into him; she usually saw him every day—in the halls or at lunch. She waited for him for half an hour at lunchtime, but he didn't show up.

"Maybe he's being mobbed, too, and can't get away," she thought, forcing herself to be optimistic.

Then, as she was collecting her books to go home, a group of students—along with Andy—crowded around Christine. They yelled cheers for the two heroes. She smiled with relief. But Andy didn't look at her. Instead he mumbled something about catching a bus and then pushed through the crowd to hurry away. Stunned, Chris watched him go. Baffled and hurt, she grabbed her book bag and ran to catch her own bus.

When she got home that afternoon, she was exhausted and even more depressed than she'd been at school. Her only hope was that by the next day, there would be some other news, to capture everyone's attention. Then maybe she could concentrate on finding Andy.

Tuesday, Wednesday, and Thursday passed in a daze for Christine. She was constantly hounded by curious class mates and had started hiding out in the school library for peace and quiet. But the peace and quiet allowed her fears about Andy to come crowding in on her again. She hadn't said a word to him since Friday. Everything had seemed so hopeful then, so happy. But not anymore. Christine didn't know why, but Andy must have lied to her when he'd said he loved her. There was no other explanation for it.

On Thursday evening Christine was sitting

on her bed. She was staring at the picture of herself and Andy, and her heart was breaking. The sight of Andy's arm around her shoulders, and the familiar backdrop of the cage caused tears to spill down her cheeks. She heard footsteps outside the door. Quickly, she hid the photograph inside her book and wiped her eyes as her mother came into her room.

"Want to tell me what's wrong?"

Christine put down the book she had been pretending to read, and looked into her mother's warm, green eyes. How she wished those eyes that were looking at her with such love were Andy's instead of her mother's. "Oh, Mom!" she said. "Nothing turned out the way I expected it to." She let herself be rocked in a comforting hug. But the heartache didn't go away.

"Is it Andy, sweetheart? He hasn't called you, has he?"

Christine gave a short laugh. "How can you always read my mind, Mom?" She sat back and pushed her hair out of her face. "I don't know why, but he hasn't even said hello to me all week. It's just that—I don't know. He should have called, or something . . ." She trailed off, shaking her head.

"Have you tried to call him?"

"Why, what's the use?" Chris sniffed, feeling utterly hopeless. "He obviously doesn't like me."

Mrs. Harter shook her head. "Oh, honey. Give him a chance. Maybe he's a lot shyer than you think. Just go up to him and say, 'Hey, Andy. Want to solve a crime?' It's easy."

Chris lowered her eyes, thinking that maybe her mother really didn't understand, after all. She shrugged. "Maybe."

Her mother stood up. "Well, I think you'd be pretty crazy to give up without a fight."

At lunch on Friday, Christine decided she would hide out in the library again—she could always eat something when she got home. Taking a seat at a table in the corner, she stared out the window. She tried to force herself to think, to decide whether or not she should track Andy down to confront him.

Suddenly a small, flat box tied with a ribbon appeared on the table in front of her. She took it without looking up.

"Open it," Andy said.

She slowly pulled off the ribbon and removed the top of the box. Nestled inside, under some tissue paper, was a small, brass-handled magnifying glass. She sniffed, feeling those tears come to her eyes.

Pulling out a chair, Andy sat down next to her, and took her hand. She finally looked at him. His eyes were tender and warm as he looked into hers.

"Why didn't you call?" she whispered, her chin quivering dangerously. "Why have you avoided me all week?"

He opened his mouth to speak, but stopped himself as if he was trying to find the right words. He sighed and started again. "Christine, I'm sorry. I know it was unfair of me. But last weekend—Friday night—scared me. I felt, I don't know. Finding out that Keeler was the thief and that he might have been trying to frame me. Well, that was pretty hard to handle. It's taken me all this time to convince myself that just because I made one mistake, doesn't mean I shouldn't trust anybody."

Christine looked silently into his eyes as he went on. "And that's just it. I realized on Friday night how strongly I felt—I feel—about you. But then I thought, 'Maybe you're wrong again.' " He looked so frightened and unsure of himself that Christine's heart went out to him. "Don't you see? I just couldn't take it if I was wrong about you, too."

He looked away quickly and swallowed hard. Turning back he finished, "Do you know how scary and confusing it is to think you can't trust someone you know you love?"

Vividly remembering the fears that she had had when she'd thought that Andy was the thief, Christine half laughed, half sighed. "I do. I know exactly what you mean." She looked down at his hand on hers and finally felt happy and sure. "But this is real, Andy. Really." Her conviction drove the fears away, and she looked into his face. She was sure she loved him.

Her certainty seemed to get rid of his fears, too, and he smiled his old, brilliant smile. Andy's eyes sparkled with happiness. "I know that now, Christine. I really do."

They were silent for a moment, gazing at each other. Then Andy winked. "Maybe we should start all over, huh? No more secret meetings in locker rooms. No more suspecting each other of being the criminal OK? Let's try something normal like going to the movies, and stuff like that."

Christine laughed. "But I meet all the best people in locker rooms." She picked up the magnifying glass. "What's this for, anyway? Tracking footprints, like Sherlock Holmes?" she asked feeling light and bouyant.

Standing and taking the glass from her, he

held it up to one eye and said, "No. It's for keeping me under surveillance." He put the magnifying glass down on the table, pulled her up, and took her in his arms. "All the time."